QUEEN OF THE COLD-BLOODED TALES

QUEEN OF THE COLD-BLOODED TALES

Roberta Simpson Brown

August House Publishers, Inc.
LITTLE ROCK

Published by August House, Inc.,
P.O. Box 3223, Little Rock, Arkansas, 72203,
501-372-5450.

Printed in the United States of America

10 9 8 7 6 5 4 3 2

LIBRARY OF CONGRESS CATALOGING-IN-PUBLICATION DATA

Brown, Roberta Simpson, 1939-
The queen of the cold-blooded tales / Roberta Simpson Brown
p. cm.
ISBN 0-87483-332-9 (hb: alk. paper) :
1. Horror tales, American. I. Title.
[PS3552.R699Q44 1993]
813'.54—dc20 93-19538

Executive: Liz Parkhurst
Project editor: Kathleen Harper
Design director: Ted Parkhurst
Cover design: Wendell E. Hall
Typography: Peerless Lettergraphics

This book is printed on archival-quality paper which meets the guidelines for performance and durability of the Committee on Production Guidelines for Book Longevity of the Council on Library Resources.

AUGUST HOUSE, INC. PUBLISHERS LITTLE ROCK

This book is dedicated to my husband, Lonnie, whose music, kindness, and joy of living touches the lives of all he meets, and keeps the bad things away.

Acknowledgments

Special thanks to all the staff at August House, especially Liz and Ted Parkhurst and Kathleen Harper. Their help and encouragement can't be measured.

To the late Ted Parkhurst, Sr., whose wit, help, and kindness Lonnie and I will never forget.

To many members of my family who helped me one way or another while I was writing my stories: Tom and Lillian Simpson; Fatima, Ervin, Mike, Scott, and Susan Atchley; Lonnie, Lena, Charlie, and Vicki Brown.

To Vicki Brown for thinking of the title "Skin Crawlers."

To super dog Howard, who stayed by my side while I was writing and kept me on task.

To those who did extra promotions: Deanna Hansen, Gail Moody, Charlene Cornell, John Ferguson, Mary Hamilton, and Norma Lewis.

To Suzi Stuart Cederholm Schuhmann for her special coaching, consultations, promotions, and support!

To all who bought my first book, *The Walking Trees and Other Scary Stories,* and made it a success.

Contents

Introduction

Since August House published my first book, *The Walking Trees and Other Scary Stories*, I have often been asked why I think such stories are of value. I have decided to include some of the answers here from my roles as a listener, a storyteller, a teacher, and an author.

As a listener, I grew up on a Kentucky farm at the edge of Appalachia, where telling scary stories was an exciting form of entertainment. To me, they became more than that. I could put myself into a scary story, experience and face up to fear in a safe, controlled situation, and try to overcome it. It was a practice run for reality! It gave me confidence that I could transfer to real things and fearful situations that I couldn't control.

When I became a professional storyteller, I realized that one thing all human beings have in common is the powerful emotion of fear. I saw that scary stories grabbed the attention of the most reluctant listener. When I look out at the huge audiences that come to hear ghost tales, I am convinced that people have a need to share fear and realize that they are not alone.

When I am teaching in workshops or in my classroom, I use scary stories to encourage people not to let their fear grow into vague, unknown things. Isolate it! Identify it! Draw a picture of it or give it a name; learn all about it and share it. This leads to reading, critical thinking, discussions, and writing and telling stories. Those skills inspired by scary stories are of tremendous value!

Few of the stories I write have happy endings. This is *not* because I think evil always wins over good. I don't think that at all. I do believe that we live in a scary world and I think a little fear gives us a healthy edge for surviving in it.

My stories are about familiar things and dark, different aspects of modern life. They are not meant to make anyone be afraid all the time, but I hope they will be reminders that dangerous situations, people, and things are out there and that it is important to recognize them and be alert.

I hope my stories will cause parents and teachers and children to talk about things that they fear and the fact that it is okay to be afraid. Through scary stories, we can all learn to live with fear comfortably.

If you have no one to hear your scary story, write to me! I'll always be glad to listen and I'll value what you say.

—Roberta Simpson Brown
Louisville, Kentucky

Skin Crawlers

June Patterson's skin crawled as she stood at the beginning of the trail, holding her flashlight and waiting for the campers to assemble for the night hike. Something had just slithered through the weeds near her foot, and it filled her with foreboding. She felt like a little girl again, imagining that hideous things were hiding in the dark.

She wasn't particularly fond of these outings, but she needed the extra income she earned from the camp for school, since her late father's estate had not made adequate provisions for her. He had, in fact, died broke. She had to work to be able to stay in school.

She didn't hate working and she didn't hate the outdoors in general; she just really hated snakes. She had her father to thank for that. She wondered if he had any idea of what he had done to her, or if he even cared. It didn't matter now anyway. All that was in the past. She was grateful, though, that she hadn't seen any snakes around camp so far.

She heard the slithering again in the weeds and began to picture a long line of snakes coiled along the trail waiting to strike.

"Serpents are everywhere!" her father use to tell her.

The thought prompted a warning.

"Watch where you're walking," she cautioned the campers as they started off up the trail. "We don't want any snakebites."

Norman Winfrey, bringing up the rear of the line, grinned to himself as he remembered the look on Miss June's face when a frog had hopped out of the weeds by the lake the first day of camp.

The counselors had been instructing Norman and the other campers about the camp's boating rules, when Norman spotted the frog. He'd welcomed the diversion. Frogs were much more interesting than rules to Norman.

He hadn't seen Miss June standing nearby when he'd grabbed at the frog, but he'd heard her gasp when she'd seen the movement in the weeds. He'd watched her stand absolutely petrified until the frog emerged.

She'd let out a cry of relief and had spoken aloud to herself in a trembling voice.

"It's just a frog!" she'd said. "It's not a snake, thank goodness."

Norman had smiled.

"She's afraid of snakes," he'd realized.

Norman was glad she was scared. She'd picked on him for no reason ever since he'd stepped off the bus. He filed his knowledge of her fear in the back of his mind to use if he had a chance to get even in the future.

Norman's dislike for Miss June had grown in the days that followed. She was always finding fault with him for something.

He was at the back of the line now because he wanted to put as much distance between Miss June and himself as he possibly could.

The night hikers followed the trail by the lake, swung up the hill by the old cemetery, and then began the descent through the woods along a rough path that led back to camp. The whole thing had taken about forty-five minutes. Some of the younger campers were already getting tired or frightened and were requiring a little extra attention.

June Patterson walked right by the small, dark hole without noticing it. She also didn't see the small, naughty boy at the back of the line stop to examine it.

Norman's eye had caught a quick movement, so he had knelt by the hole and stuck his hand inside. He was thrilled to touch something cold and slimy.

He carefully grasped the squirming body and pulled it out into the moonlight. He was delighted. It was like nothing he had ever seen before. It looked more like a snake than anything else, but its color was a blazing red and it had sharp teeth. It didn't try to bite him, though.

He couldn't risk a closer examination because his flashlight might attract too much attention. They weren't suppose to turn them on unless it was absolutely necessary, and he'd already had his on too long.

He snapped off the light and stood in the dark, holding the wiggling thing in his hand, thinking how much fun he could have with it. Best of all, he knew it would send Miss June into fits. He would have to give some thought to what he could do with it to scare her the most. His thoughts were interrupted by her voice.

"Norman Winfrey, what on earth are you doing back there?" she wanted to know.

Norman realized that the group had stopped, waiting for him. He saw Miss June take a few steps toward him, so he quickly stuffed his catch down in his knapsack.

"I'm sorry, Miss June," he said in a syrupy voice that was obviously insincere.

Even though the moonlight was strong, June hadn't actually seen what happened. She wasn't sure she wanted to know. She was certain that whatever it was, it was not in her best interest. The hike continued, but June kept an eye on Norman the rest of the way. He did nothing else to arouse her suspicion.

As soon as they arrived back at camp, Miss June directed all the campers to prepare for bed at once. Norman was the last one to begin.

"Put that knapsack away, Norman," she ordered. "And make sure you clean it out. I don't want some creature crawling into my bed tonight."

For once, Norman obeyed without arguing. That in itself was enough to make her suspect that he was up to something. She doubted that he had cleaned everything out of the knapsack, but she and Norman both knew that she would not have the courage to check it.

For Norman, obeying had been easy this time. He had left the creature in the bottom of the knapsack, but he had no intention of doing anything so obvious as putting it in her bed that night. He wasn't that stupid. He'd thought of something better. He was going to wait until she was ready to go into town, and then he was going to slip it inside her van. He could picture the wild ride when she discovered it. He wished he could be along, but he doubted that that would be possible. Seeing the results would be enough.

The idea excited him. He wanted to get another look at his captive up close. Maybe he could figure out what it was. If not, he'd ask somebody later. Right now it was wiser to keep it a secret.

Norman waited until everyone was asleep and all the lights were out. He reached under the bed and pulled out his knapsack. He eased his hand inside and gasped. It was empty! He took his flashlight and shined it all around the floor. There was nothing there.

At that same moment, a shriek came from the girls' cabin. The shriek became a chorus of howls that brought everyone in camp scrambling out of bed.

June ran to her window, expecting to see Norman in the midst of the uproar. Instead he was at the door of his cabin, right where he should be.

As Norman watched Miss June race the short distance from her place to the girls' cabin, he saw a red flash streak from the girls' window and disappear in the bushes.

Still holding his knapsack, he dashed to the bushes and parted them carefully. The red creature lay quietly on the ground, looking up at him. It offered no resistance as he picked it up and gently placed it back in the knapsack.

Norman moved over by Miss June's van to see if he could hear what had happened.

The girls had stopped screeching and were fairly quiet now. Everybody was gathered around, listening to them tell about something with red teeth that had crawled toward their beds. Their noise had frightened it away, so nobody had actually been hurt.

June remembered the incident on the trail with Norman.

"Tell Norman Winfrey that I want to talk to him right now," she told one of the campers.

The camper saw Norman at the van and gave him the message. Norman had heard her and was already trying to decide what to do. He hadn't meant to put the snake-like thing in her van just yet, but he couldn't let her find him with it. He ducked around back and dumped the contents of his knapsack through the open window. Then he reported to Miss June, carrying the empty knapsack with him.

"I thought you might want to see this," he said innocently, holding it out to her.

She shuddered and felt skin crawlers all over her body again.

"Tell me what you put in that knapsack on the hike," she demanded.

"Nothing," Norman replied. "See?"

He opened the knapsack and turned it so she could see inside.

"I know there is nothing in there now," she said. "But I also know that something was there, and whatever it was, it got out and crawled in here. It might have hurt the girls. I want you to search until you find it."

She appointed several other boys to help Norman look.

They turned up nothing and soon began to grumble about not getting to sleep. June Patterson decided they all might as well go back to bed. The thing was probably gone for good, anyway.

Again Norman waited until everyone was asleep. Then he got up and headed for the van. Maybe putting the thing in there wasn't such a good idea after all. She'd know for sure that he did it, and he'd get blamed if she had a wreck when she saw it. He decided to take it out and leave it on the trail where he had found it.

He reached the van and peered inside. The red thing was there, glowing eerily in the moonlight. Norman reached down to pick it up.

This time it hissed as soon as he touched it. The angry sound filled the whole van and shocked Norman. He jumped back, but he felt the teeth clamp down. He struggled, but they held firm and Norman could feel spurts of hot liquid shoot into his hand.

It released its hold, and he flung the thing to the floor. It darted under the seat in a flash of red.

Norman tried to stay calm and think of what he should do. He examined the bite, but it didn't look too bad. He didn't feel sick. If the thing had been poisonous, surely he would be feeling some effects by now. He didn't dare tell anyone. Then Miss June would find out that he brought the thing to camp. As soon as she knew for sure, she'd punish him.

He walked back to his cabin, quietly so as not to wake the others, and took some ointment from his first aid kit and rubbed it on the bite. Then he went to bed.

At dawn the commotion in the boys' cabin woke June Patterson with a start. She wasted no time in reaching the source of the uproar.

The boys fell silent when she came in. They had been clustered around Norman's bed, but they stepped back to let her through.

She cringed when she saw him. He lay unconscious with his arm flung across the bed. Red streaks were running up from his hand and they were raised in ridges. The worst part was the way the ridges were moving. It looked like something was crawling under his skin.

In one swift movement, she pulled a blanket around him and lifted him in her arms. She ran to her van and the others followed, one boy even having the presence of mind to open the door for her.

"I've got to get him to the hospital," she said. "I'll have to count on you to stay in your cabins until I get back."

They nodded, frightened and silent, and moved away as she started the van and backed into the road.

June had never been so frightened in her life. She tried to concentrate on the road, but her attention was divided between driving and looking at the still form on the seat beside her. He looked so vulnerable. He was only a boy, not an enemy. Why hadn't she tried harder to understand him?

She cleared the entrance ramp on the interstate and headed toward the hospital exit a few miles away.

At first, she didn't hear the rustling in the back. She was going over and over last night in her mind. Why hadn't she insisted that they keep looking until they found that awful thing? It was all her fault. She had been too terrified that it was a snake to take a look in the knapsack. Now the boy might die because she had been a coward.

She drove faster, hoping she could get to the hospital in time to save him.

She tried to pinpoint the time when she had seen Norman last. It must have been around 1:00 A.M. He had to have been bitten after that. Now it was about 7:15 A.M. He could have been in this condition for about six hours. She wondered how much time he had left.

Her exit was coming up next. Ahead, she could see the traffic slowing down. There must have been an accident. She couldn't afford a delay, but she had no choice but to bring the van to a stop.

That was when she first noticed the rustling. She looked over her shoulder and caught a glimpse of something red moving on the floor. She hadn't felt such panic since she was a child, and her father used to lock her in her room when she was disobedient and turn snakes loose. She could still hear his drunken laugh when she pleaded with him to let her out and promised to be good.

"Serpents are everywhere!" she could hear him hiss at her. The cruelty in his voice was something she could never forget.

Traffic was inching ahead now, so she concentrated on maneuvering the van onto the shoulder of the road and then down the exit ramp.

She was on the street at last, but the traffic light a block from the hospital caught her. She heard the rustling on the floor again and looked around, but she couldn't see anything. Maybe her eyes had been playing tricks on her before.

She turned back to see if the light had changed, and just then, something red flashed over the back of the seat and struck her arm. She thought for an instant that it was the red traffic light she had seen, and that she'd only bumped her arm. Then she felt the teeth sinking into her arm and puncturing her veins. She could feel spurts of hot liquid surging from the thing into her body.

She shot through the light and turned into the emergency entrance, all the time screaming hysterically and shaking her arm to get the sleek red thing to let go. She hit the brake and the van skidded up against the curb. June fainted and fell against the horn. The red thing slipped to the floor and disappeared.

When she woke up, June was in a hospital bed. Slowly, her mind cleared and she remembered why she had come here. She tried to sit up, but she was dizzy. A nurse hurried over.

"Where's the boy?" June cried. "Norman Winfrey. What is wrong with him?"

"Try to be calm and rest," the nurse answered.

"I want to know about the boy!" June insisted.

"He's in surgery right now," said the nurse.

"Why?" asked June. "Tell me what's wrong!"

"I can't tell you what bit him, but I assure you that everything that can be done is being done."

"I want to see him," said June.

She threw back the sheet and that's when she saw them—the raised red streaks running up her arm, crawling under her skin.

June pushed the nurse aside and ran into the hall. She could hear the nurse coming after her, but she managed to stay just ahead. She hesitated only long enough to read the signs. She burst through the doors marked SURGERY—NO ADMITTANCE. She stopped abruptly when she saw the scene before her.

Norman Winfrey lay on the table, writhing in pain under the straps that held him down. The red streaks on his arms were bulging now, and as June watched along with the horrified doctors and nurses, the streaks burst open and out came small, red, snake-like creatures with rows of little teeth. As they squirmed off the table and crawled away, Norman's body shed its skin and it fell to the floor.

Unearthly screams tore from Norman's throat, his body convulsed, and then he lay still.

For a second, no one moved. Then panic shattered the frozen tableau, and suddenly the room was in chaos.

The nurse grabbed June and pulled her into the hall. She swayed, then leaned against the nurse for support.

Norman's screams had sounded exactly like her father's screams the last time she saw him. He had died shaking, swearing that serpents were biting him and driving him mad. The doctors had said it was from the alcohol. Now she wasn't sure.

She looked down at her arms. The streaks were growing. In less than six hours, she'd die like poor little Norman Winfrey. Maybe she'd go mad first like her father. She could already hear voices hissing in her ears.

Other voices were whispering nearby. The doctors stood by the surgery door, shaken and pale.

"They're gone," she heard one say. "They shot out like red hot flames, and then they just died out. I couldn't tell you where they went."

June tried to tell them, but the pain made it impossible to speak. The secret would die with her and Norman if she didn't reveal it, but she was on fire inside. The inner voices hissed and laughed and leaped at her like hot flames.

She surrendered to the darkness and felt herself melting into the pain.

Off the interstate by the camp near the lake, little red flashes darted into a small dark hole by a rough path in the woods near an old cemetery. The earth absorbed the heat, and the little bodies became cold and slimy.

June's last thought was about the awful truth of her father's words. Indeed, the serpents were everywhere.

The Tractor

Arthur Blake watched the little boy cross the campground and walk past the sign to the section marked OFF LIMITS. He headed straight to the barn, just as Arthur knew he would. Arthur figured it would take him about four minutes to reach the barn on his short legs.

Arthur chuckled when he thought of how he'd look to that boy. He knew how much he had deteriorated in the last few years, but he didn't care. If his appearance scared the boy, then so be it! He had no business coming here. Arthur belonged in this barn more than anyone else did. He wasn't forcing anyone to come look at him.

Nobody had cared about what happened to Arthur. He didn't think he should have to be concerned about anyone now.

Arthur had been coming back as often as he could to look at what had once been his. He missed the tractor most of all. Riding on it, plowing the land that had been in his family for four generations, gave him a sense of security and power over his own destiny.

Now that was gone. Somehow he had lost control. How did it happen? What could he have done differently? Why did he keep trying to hold on to his old life by coming back and sitting on that rusty old tractor again and again?

He wasn't sure of the answers. How could he be? He was just the shadow of the man he used to be, sitting inside an old barn watching a curious little boy approaching to peek inside.

Strangers like this boy were swarming all over the place now, and there was nothing he could do about it. Well, not much anyway.

"I have nobody to blame but myself," he thought. But that was not true.

The state of the economy was mainly at fault. All farmers had been hit hard that year. Many had lost their farms, just like Arthur Blake.

The year before, Arthur had been forced to take a mortgage on the farm to buy some expensive equipment he needed. Combines did not come cheap. Neither did his new tractor. He'd had no problem making the payments until a series of financial catastrophes struck. A spring storm ripped off a section of his barn roof. Continuing heavy rains kept the ground too wet for planting until way past the appropriate time. When the rains stopped, a summer drought caused the crops to fail for the first time in years. Arthur had no money to make the mortgage payments. He spent many sleepless nights going over his accounts before the bank foreclosed.

Never had he felt anything as deeply as the pain he felt at losing his farm and his self-respect. It had all been entrusted to him, and he had failed. He had to take his family and leave.

He sat on his tractor a long time that day before he went about relocating his family.

From then on, Arthur Blake's life was over. Farming was all he knew and all he wanted to know. He couldn't live with the thought of anyone else having his land.

He thought about what happened to old Abner Remington and his family. Horrible as it was, it was exactly what Abner deserved. Not his family, maybe, but certainly Abner! Arthur's family hadn't deserved to have their lives destroyed, either, but the innocent had to suffer along with the guilty.

Abner Remington was the local banker who had approved the foreclosure on Arthur's mortgage. Then, as soon as the land went up for sale, Abner bought it as a home for his only daughter and her family. With his wife dead, he wanted them nearby. His son-in-law did not approve, but Abner ignored him.

"The Lord knows," Abner told everybody, "my son-in-law could never be able to afford a decent place for my daughter and grandson without my help."

"You helped yourself to my land," thought Arthur. "You could have extended my loan, but you refused because you wanted my farm for yourself. Now you have meddled in your son-in-law's business. Believe me, old man, you'll live to regret it!"

The son-in-law swallowed his pride and moved his family to the farm. He'd never farmed before, but decided to give it a try. He began to like it.

Day after day he worked the fields on the tractor that had once belonged to Arthur Blake. People began to think that the old farm might flourish again—everyone except Arthur.

He had given lots of thought to what would make Abner suffer the most. His own situation had given him the answer. He came up with a plan. All he had to do was to find an opportunity to put it into action.

Arthur saw his chance late one afternoon. He was in the barn when Abner arrived to have dinner with his family. He kept out of sight and watched Abner greet his grandson. Arthur smiled because Abner had no inkling of what was going to happen.

To Abner it seemed like an ordinary day. The boy always greeted him first when he came to visit. Then his daughter would come out and call them to eat. The boy would go to the field to tell his father that dinner was ready.

Arthur knew the routine, too. He'd observed Abner's visits before.

As for Abner, whenever he felt a twinge of guilt about his part in taking Arthur's land, he reminded himself of how well his grandson was thriving on the farm. Tonight was such a night, and he looked forward to the evening with his family around him.

"Wash up for dinner," his daughter said as she came out to welcome him.

"I'll go get Daddy," said the boy, running to the field while his mother and grandfather stood in the yard watching him go.

"Be careful," his mother called. "Your father can't always see you from up there."

The warning came too late.

The tractor was headed to the barn as the boy darted toward it. He was being careful until Arthur appeared in the barn door. The distraction caused the boy to turn his head to see who was there. Startled by what he saw, the boy tripped and fell. Sitting high on the tractor, the father did not see his son fall, nor did he hear him cry out over the roar of the engine.

The young mother raced to her child, but her frantic attempt failed to save him. Both were caught by the tractor's wheels.

Abner watched as his son-in-law felt the bump and looked down. He saw him jump to the ground and kneel beside the still bodies. Abner tried to run to them, but he couldn't move.

The tractor, which seemed to have been blocked by something—perhaps the bodies themselves—began to move on its own. Abner could only stand helplessly by and watch as his son-in-law fell to the ground by the others.

It all happened so fast, Abner could not believe it. He replayed the accident a thousand times in his mind, but still it didn't seem true. He saw one image over and over, but he couldn't tell the police. They'd think he was crazy, and maybe he was, but he was sure he had seen Arthur Blake on the tractor when it roared to life.

With his family gone, Abner put the land up for sale. When a buyer was found, Abner took to his bed. He cried out Arthur's name and swore he was at the foot of his bed until the day he died.

The new landowner was an investor from New Hampshire who turned the farm into a campground. It was a perfect place. Business thrived in spite of reports that Arthur Blake was seen hanging around the barn.

Arthur didn't like the campground. He thought the land should be put to better use. He had an idea that he thought might work. He might be able to drive them all away at the same time.

He would start with the next overnight sleepout. One was scheduled for the Boy Scouts the next night.

There were a lot more boys than Arthur had expected. He was afraid they might all stay together near the road, and was relieved when one scout master took his troop to the field where the deaths had occurred. Arthur could see them from the barn, but they couldn't see him.

The boys and the scout master ate and sang and went to bed. They had just started to doze off when they heard something coming. It was on them before they knew it, and there was no time to get out of the way.

When they did not return to the main group the next morning, another troop went looking for them. Underneath the tents, they found all the bodies, mashed and broken. Prints of a tractor's tires were all around the tents, but no tracks led up or away.

The owner designated the fields around the old barn off-limits. Arthur watched them put up the sign. It was all he could do to hold his mad laughter silent in his throat.

After the mysterious deaths, few ventured into the restricted area, so Arthur had more freedom to come and go without being seen.

Sometimes, though, a camper would become fascinated by the stories of the killer tractor and come to take a look. Arthur tried to give such adventurers a sight to remember.

The little boy Arthur had been waiting for had crossed the forbidden field and reached the barn door now. He opened it just a crack and looked inside. He glanced first at the barn loft, and then below to where the tractor was parked—and then he saw Arthur.

Without a word, Arthur reached out and started the tractor's engine.

The boy's mouth flew open, first in surprise and then in terror. He turned on his short legs and ran for his life back across the field.

Arthur laughed to himself and climbed off the tractor. Then he left the barn and set off down the road to the place where he'd relocated his family.

He remembered vividly that awful day when he realized there was no hope. He hadn't known what to do or where he'd go. He was sitting on his tractor when something clicked inside his head and gave him the answer to his problems.

He'd called to his wife and son to come to the field. Both had hurried to see what he wanted. Then he'd started the tractor and steered it toward them, and he hadn't stopped. He'd crushed them to death before throwing himself under those gigantic wheels.

Arthur wished he could sleep as peacefully as they did, but he knew he never would. All he could do was go back and lie beside them in his grave, until it was time for another ride on his tractor.

Flower Child

"She always knows who's going to die next," Clair Burton said to her sister Katie. "How do you suppose she does that?"

"Why, Clair!" said Katie. "What a dreadful thing to say! She doesn't always know. It's just a coincidence."

"Coincidences don't happen all the time," said Clair. "I tell you, she is a strange one, even if she is our relative."

"Oh, Clair," said Katie, with a weary voice that revealed they'd had this conversation before. "You just don't like Cousin Rose."

"Well, you're right about that," said Clair. "But that doesn't change the fact that she *is* strange."

"I think she's a dear little thing," said Katie defensively.

"I don't know how you can say that," said Clair. "She broke Aunt Polly's heart when she ran off to California with that hippie. He never did marry her, you know. I think she got mixed up with some kind of cult out there and learned some strange powers."

"She just grows flowers and sells them," said Katie. "What is so strange about that?"

"She never comes around the family, except before one of them dies. She manages to show up with one of her flowers just before death comes, and she walks off with her choice of the family heirlooms every time," said Clair.

"I didn't say she's a thief," Clair pointed out. "But just look at all the things she's gotten from the family. When Uncle John died, Cousin Rose was at his bedside with a potted plant before any of the rest of us even knew he was sick. And she ended up with his entire coin collection."

"Oh, Clair, you know she always liked Uncle John. He wanted her to have his coins because she was always visiting him and bringing him flowers," said Katie.

"What about Uncle George then?" asked Clair. "She never visited him except just before he died. She arrived with a handful of violets, and he left her enough money to remodel that fancy greenhouse where she spends most of her time. Heaven only knows what she does in there."

"I'll admit that she does show up before our relatives die," said Katie, "but I don't think there is anything sinister about it."

"I would like to know what she has in that greenhouse," said Clair. "Do you know there is a section of that remodeled part where nobody is allowed? Jean Cunningham sent her gardener over there to buy some mums, and he told Jean that section was blocked off and locked. Now you have to admit that's odd."

"What's odd about that?" asked Katie. "Maybe she is growing a prize specimen to enter in the garden show, and she didn't want Jean Cunningham's gardener to see it."

"Go ahead and defend her," pouted Clair. "But just remember that she was over here last week bringing rose bushes and looking at that diamond brooch Grandmother Burton left to you. I hope you weren't fool enough to tell her she could have that just because she brought you a few flowers!"

"Clair, I'm just not up to continuing this discussion," sighed Katie. "I asked Cousin Rose to bring me the roses for our garden. She is dropping by in the morning to give me some advice. The petals are drooping, and I'm sure she'll know what to do. Think whatever you want, but leave me out of it. Now, if you will excuse me, I am going to lie down. I'm feeling a bit droopy myself."

"Of course, dear," said Clair. "Get some rest."

Clair sat on the porch for a while longer after her sister went inside. She hadn't meant to upset Katie. Katie was all the close family she had. The conversation had gotten out of hand. Perhaps she had been too hard on Cousin Rose, but she couldn't shake the feelings she had about her. Death followed wherever she went, and now she had started coming here. She'd have to be nice to Cousin Rose tomorrow for Katie's sake, unless she could think of some way to avoid meeting her at all.

"Why, I know what I'll do!" she thought. "I'll tell Katie that I am going to walk into town and shop. Then I'll walk over by Cousin Rose's greenhouse while she's visiting Katie! Maybe I can sneak a look into that section that she's got locked up."

Once she had decided, she could hardly wait for morning.

Katie was still feeling tired the next morning, but she was up and dressed for Cousin Rose's visit. She didn't protest when Clair announced that she had some errands to do in town.

As Clair left, she met Rose coming up the walk.

"Good morning, Clair," said Rose. "Have I come at a bad time?"

"No, Rose," said Clair. "I thought I'd take care of some business in town while you were good enough to keep Katie company."

"I'll be glad to," Rose said sweetly.

"Then I'll be on my way," said Clair.

Clair hurried straight to the greenhouse. She wasn't surprised to find it open. She went past the mums and the snapdragons to the locked section in the back.

"There must be a key," she said to herself.

She ran her hand along the top of the door, but there was nothing there. Then she spotted a stone beside a potted plant, and raised it up. The key was underneath. Her hand shook as she inserted it in the lock and turned it. She slowly opened the door and stepped in.

This part of the greenhouse was definitely different! It was much hotter than the main section. There was something else that she couldn't quite distinguish at first. Then it came to her. It was the smell. In the main section, the flowers smelled fresh and sweet. This part smelled of damp earth and funeral flowers. She was almost overcome by what she saw in front of her. She had walked into a house of death. Pots of flowers were arranged in rows like mourners in pews. In the middle of the floor was a single pot that drew Clair's attention. It contained the largest, whitest rose that Clair had ever seen.

She was awed as she approached it. There was no denying that it was more beautiful than any flower she had ever imagined. She had no idea where such a flower could have come from or why Rose had it locked away. She wanted to look closer, but her heart pounded with every step she took. In the middle of the hot greenhouse, she began to shiver. Why did she feel surrounded by evil in the presence of such beauty? She forced herself to walk to the rare specimen and look at the petals. Then she screamed and ran from the greenhouse as she had never run before in her life.

She thought her lungs would burst, but she didn't stop. She had to get home. She had to get to her sister! Deep down she knew it was useless, but maybe, maybe, there was some way to save her.

As she came in sight of the house, she saw Dr. Miller's car. She knew what she would find.

Katie was on the couch with Cousin Rose beside her when Clair rushed in.

"Katie!" cried Clair. "What's happened to you?"

Clair reached out and took Katie's hand. It was cold and clammy. Her voice was very weak when she spoke.

"Now, don't worry, Clair," she said. "I'm just a little tired. All I need is to rest for a while."

"You need to rest, too," said Rose. "I'll sit with her while you catch your breath."

Rose's voice drew Clair's attention. She thought her eyes were deceiving her. The diamond brooch was pinned to Rose's dress.

Clair wanted to rip it from her dress and throw her out the door.

"Where did you get that?" she demanded.

It was Katie's voice that answered.

"I hope you won't mind that I gave Grandmother Burton's brooch to Rose, Clair. We have so many of her things, and Cousin Rose has nothing of hers."

Clair was shaking with rage, but she couldn't risk upsetting Katie.

Dr. Miller touched her shoulder.

"Come outside with me so Katie can get some rest," he said.

Clair followed him to the screened porch.

"It's her heart," he said to Clair. "I doubt that she'll last the day. There is nothing we can do but make her comfortable. Please don't do anything to upset her. Your Cousin Rose has offered to stay and help. Katie told me that you don't like Rose, but I hope you'll think of Katie's condition and stay as calm as you can."

Clair stood there trembling. It was too late to save her sister. He'd never believe her about Rose. It was too late to tell him how Rose always knew who would die next. It was too late to describe what she'd seen in the locked section of the greenhouse or to tell him about the white rose—the rose with Katie Burton's face etched in the petals. It was too late, because even as she had started to run from the greenhouse, Clair had seen that the petals were closing.

Sleeping Bags

The breeze was light, but the tall branches swayed in it, beckoning Susan Ackerly to follow the sign that said, THREE MILES TO CAMP STONE HILL. She turned the radio on and tried several stations, but all she got was static or silence. She must be out of range. That seemed odd. Surely there was at least one local station. She gave up and turned the radio off.

The road dipped into a little valley dotted with color. She was surprised to see so many flowers here. She'd heard too many church songs about dark, lonesome valleys.

They had given her flowers when she left home today. Now they lay on the seat near the sleeping bag. She'd had lots of flowers at the hospital, too, after her accident. They'd made her room smell good.

As Susan turned onto the narrow road that wound through the trees, the light breeze turned into a strong wind, whipping the limbs low toward the ground. She smelled damp, rotting wood and felt the air turn colder. The sun was setting, and the sky that showed in patches through the leaves was growing darker by the minute.

Trees had taken on a sinister quality since her accident. She had driven her car into one in a storm just about this same time of day.

She wondered if she'd feel the effects of her accident at camp. She hoped not. She hoped that all of that was behind her now. Maybe at camp she'd at least get over cringing at the sight of trees.

Nobody at home had wanted her to come here. She hadn't wanted to come at first herself, but she thought it was a good idea now. Anyway, it was too late to go back.

She could hear a far-off wailing behind her. The wind must be picking up.

Seeing the growing shadows, Susan began to feel anxious. She wanted to reach camp before dark, because she was uneasy about driving on these bumpy, dirt roads in the woods at night. The prospect of sleeping alone in such an isolated location didn't appeal to her either. Anything could be out there in the woods.

There was one thing that had especially bothered her today. She was sure she had been followed part of the way when she left today. She didn't know how many were in the cars, because she'd only glanced back and seen them once. Then she had to look ahead. All of them had looked grim and unhappy. She had lost them a little ways back, so she knew they weren't following her now. Still, the whole thing made her uncomfortable. She'd be glad to join the others at camp tonight and get a peaceful sleep.

The car bumped over a piece of limb in the road and the sleeping bag shifted toward the passenger side. She glanced nervously at it, and then turned quickly away. Here in the woods, the bag didn't look warm and comforting. It looked like a dark mound of earth ready to swallow her up. She didn't look at it again, but gave her full attention to the road.

"This is a long three miles," she thought. "I hope I didn't miss the turn."

She was beginning to believe she had, when her headlights picked up another sign that said ENTRANCE TO CAMP STONE HILL.

In the lights, Susan could see a figure in white standing near the entrance. As she slowed and stopped, she could see that it was a girl about her own age. The girl crossed to the car and gave Susan a smile.

"Susan Ackerly?" she asked.

"Yes," said Susan.

"Well, hi, Susan," said the girl. "I'm your guide, Angie Hunter."

"I didn't know that someone would meet me," said Susan.

"We've been waiting for you," said Angie. "We were afraid you were lost."

"To tell you the truth, Angie," said Susan, "I thought I was lost once myself."

"You are the last one we expect tonight," said Angie. "I'll get in and show you where to go."

Susan reached over and opened the car door for Angie. She was relieved that she was no longer alone. She'd been more frightened than she thought, but she realized now how silly she'd been. She felt safe now, even though it had gotten very dark.

Angie leaned over and picked up the flowers from the seat. She slid the sleeping bag close to Susan and placed the flowers on top. Then she got in and closed the door.

"Pretty flowers," she said. "Too bad they don't last long. These are starting to wilt already."

"I know," said Susan. "I sometimes wonder why people spend so much money on things like that that don't last."

"They gave you a big send-off, huh?" asked Angie.

"Oh, yes," laughed Susan. "Flowers, tears, food—the works! My mother even picked out this outfit for me."

"That's nice," said Angie. "By the way, are you hungry? I can dig up something for you if you haven't eaten."

"No, thanks," said Susan. "I'll tackle soul food in the morning. Right now, I'm ready to sleep!"

"Go straight ahead," Angie directed, pointing toward a clearing among the trees.

Susan drove slowly in the direction Angie pointed until Angie motioned for her to stop. Her bumper came to rest against a tree.

The two girls sat quietly for a moment before getting out of the car. Angie gave Susan time to take in her new surroundings before she spoke.

"Be sure to bring your sleeping bag," she said.

Susan looked at the flowers and left them on the seat. She took the bag and followed Angie up a path lined with stones.

"Everyone is sleeping on the hill tonight," explained Angie. "You'll see them later."

"It was nice of you to come out and meet me," said Susan.

"No problem," said Angie. "Some of us always do it for the new ones. It can be frightening coming here alone."

"It was a bit scary," said Susan. "I'll admit I didn't know what to expect. It's so different from what I was told it would be!"

"Lots of people are surprised," said Angie.

The girls were now among stones of various shapes and sizes. Looking over Angie's shoulder, Susan could see rows of sleeping bags on the ground.

"This is your place," said Angie. "You can put your sleeping bag next to mine."

Susan untied her bag and rolled it out. The bag did not look frightening here, as it had on the car seat. Angie wasted no time getting settled in her bag, so Susan climbed into hers and settled down, too. The soft lining shrouded her with warmth.

She was sure she'd go right to sleep, but she didn't. Images of her life came and went. It was too quiet to sleep. She was used to noise—music, voices, sirens—things like that.

Stars came out and twinkled far, far above in the sky, but nobody in the sleeping bags moved.

"It feels strange," Susan whispered. "I miss the sounds."

"You'll get used to it," Angie whispered back. "Then you'll love it."

The girls lay on their backs with their hands clasped and watched the moon ease across the sky. By its light, Susan could clearly see the stones at the heads of the sleeping bags.

She read Angie's first, and then her own—the year of birth, the year of death. Angie was probably right. She would come to love the silence now that she was no longer among the living.

Threads

Connie Adams didn't think much about the first little spot of blood on the pillowcase. She assumed she had scratched herself in her sleep. She looked closely in the mirror and saw a tiny line with dried blood on the left side of her neck. She examined her hands. There was no blood on them or even under the nails.

She ran her finger along the scratch and asked herself, "I wonder how I did that?"

The blood had dried, and Connie worried that it had stained the pillowcase and maybe even the pillow. She slipped the pretty hand-embroidered case off the pillow. No blood had soaked through.

She took the pillowcase to the bathroom and turned on the cold water. Some of the blood washed away as she rubbed it gently, but there was an ugly trace of brown left on the soft material.

There was something else she noticed. Two of the threads in the embroidered lily pattern were broken. Maybe she could fix them before Matt noticed. He'd think she did it on purpose because she didn't like to use his dead wife's things.

Connie and Matt had had their first argument about these handmade bedclothes right after they were married. Connie had wanted her own things, but Matt insisted that it was silly to spend money when all these perfectly beautiful things were still in good condition. Connie protested that even the patterns stood for Lily's name, but Matt told her she was being silly.

Matt had gotten his way, as usual. Connie didn't like confrontations of any kind. It was easier to do what Matt wanted than to argue about it. Maybe it would be silly to throw out perfectly good things just because Matt's first wife had made them.

Still, it bothered Connie and she didn't feel right about sleeping on them. In fact, she had trouble going to sleep every night. The sheets were icy cold.

"Could I buy an electric blanket?" she asked Matt.

"I hate those things," he told her. "They're either too hot or too cold or the wiring doesn't work."

Connie said no more about the blanket. They continued to sleep under Lily's homemade quilts.

She pointed out another odd thing to Matt after it had happened several times.

"Neither of us toss and turn at night," she told him, "but the covers are always pushed up around our necks. Don't you think that's strange?"

"What's strange about that?" he asked.

"I'm careful to tuck them under snugly every night," she explained. "I don't know how they get around my neck!"

"You tug at them at night because of your cold nature," he said.

She didn't argue, but she didn't think the answer was as simple as that.

Connie mentioned it to her sister Jane once when they were talking. Jane had made a flippant remark of the sort that was somewhat characteristic of her.

"Maybe it's the ghost of Lily Adams trying to get even with you for stealing Matt," she teased.

Connie didn't laugh.

"I didn't steal Matt," she said. "Lily was dead before I dated Matt."

Jane had apologized and changed the subject.

Connie wondered if she should call her sister today and tell her about the scratch and the broken thread. She decided not to. She wasn't in the mood for any snide remarks from Jane about Lily's ghost. The whole thing was too spooky without that.

Connie replaced the broken threads and ironed the pillowcase before placing it back on the bed. The stain was so faint that Matt would never notice.

All that day she told herself that it wasn't important, but as she was setting the table for dinner, she noticed two broken threads in the lily design on the embroidered napkins. She quickly folded the napkins so the threads wouldn't show.

Connie nearly dropped the potatoes at dinner when she saw a scratch on Matt's neck just like hers.

She stared so long, a scowl came over Matt's face.

"What are you looking at?" he snapped.

"I'm sorry," said Connie meekly. "Did you cut yourself shaving?"

"Must've," he mumbled between bites.

He seemed annoyed with her the rest of the evening, so she found work to do in the kitchen to keep out of his way.

It was a restless night for both of them. Matt called out in his sleep and Connie woke several times, feeling something like threads on her neck.

The next morning, there was a spot of blood on the sheet between them. Lily's design was on the sheets, too, so Connie checked quickly to see if it was intact. It wasn't! Two of the threads were broken!

"Maybe the thread's old," she thought.

She had just finished repairing the stitches when a car pulled up. She was surprised to see it was Jane.

Jane always timed her visits so she wouldn't be there when Matt was home, but Connie was not expecting her today.

"Hi, Sis!" she said, sticking her head inside the doorway. "Is the ogre here?"

Connie sighed and ignored the comment. She hated being in the middle. She wished they'd get along. Connie hated confrontations.

"Come on in, Jane," she said. "Matt's at work."

"Good!" said Jane. "How about treating me to lunch?"

"If you'll settle for soup and salad," said Connie.

"Perfect," said Jane.

Connie scurried around the kitchen putting on the soup and throwing together two salads, but she kept an eye on Jane. Something was on her mind. She hoped Jane wasn't going to get started on Matt again. She didn't want to listen to Jane telling her she ought to stand up more to

Matt. Jane was too independent to understand a man like Matt. Sometimes Connie wanted to tell her that if she didn't stop looking for the perfect man, she would end up an old maid, still selling her insurance policies for a living.

Connie put the food on the table and waited for Jane to say what she'd come to say. Finally, she tapped her spoon against her bowl and looked at Connie.

"You don't look well," Jane told her. "Haven't you been sleeping?"

"I'm fine," Connie lied, but then her lip began to quiver. She blurted out the odd incidents with the blood and the broken threads.

"I guess you think I'm crazy," she finished.

Jane shook her head. Connie had expected her to laugh, but she was serious.

"The man's a jerk, Sis, or worse," she said. "Get rid of those bedclothes, or better yet, get rid of him. He should let you buy whatever you want since he got all that insurance money."

"What money?" asked Connie. "We're on a strict budget."

"You mean that he hasn't told you about the money he got when Lily died?"

"This is none of your business, Jane. I wish you'd leave us alone," said Connie.

"I just learned something that is my business," said Jane, "and I think you ought to know. My boss at the insurance company told me that Matt took out a huge insurance policy on Lily just before she died. Now, he's taken one out on you. Frankly, that worries me. I never did think that Lily accidently fell on those scissors."

Connie tried hard to shut out Jane's voice. She couldn't be telling the truth.

"You've just accused Matt of murder!" she said. "I think you'd better go!"

"I'm sorry if I've upset you, Sis. You know where I am if you need me," said Jane.

Connie watched Jane drive away. Part of her was furious about what Jane had said, and part of her was very, very frightened.

He must have a good reason for not telling her about the insurance. She should ask him straight out, but she didn't want to confront him with something like this so soon after they'd bickered over the bedclothes.

Matt could get very angry, but he couldn't be a killer. She remembered how devastated he'd been when Lily died. The poor woman had been carrying some sewing downstairs and had tripped and fallen on her scissors. Matt was a regular customer at the coffee shop where Connie worked at that time, so she could see firsthand how deeply Lily's death affected him.

Connie had never admitted it to herself before, but Lily's accident had been a blessing for her. If Lily hadn't died, Connie would probably still be working in the coffee shop. Jane, however, had told her many times that the coffee shop would have been a better fate than marriage to Matt.

A short time after Jane's visit, Matt began to act peculiar. He was moody and withdrawn, and he wouldn't tell Connie what was bothering him.

Several times, she woke up and found him sitting in the chair that faced the stairs, with only the glow of his cigarette for light.

"Are you all right?" she asked.

"Just go back to bed," he ordered, his voice more desperate than angry.

One night, Connie had been a long time falling asleep, so she was groggy when she heard the footsteps.

"Matt must be up," she thought.

She reached over, but Matt was in bed. He, too, was awake.

"What is that?" she whispered.

"Nothing!" he said. "Go back to sleep!"

The footsteps stopped when he spoke, and she didn't hear them again.

The next morning, Matt shook her awake. She couldn't understand why Matt was glaring at her.

"How long has this been going on?" he asked her.

She was confused, but she looked where he was pointing. There was another spot of blood, and this time it covered one of the fancy flowers on Matt's pillow case. Connie could see the threads were matted and broken.

"Why didn't you tell me about this?" he demanded.

"I didn't want to upset you," Connie told him.

"I'll deal with you when I get home," he raged. "I'm late for work."

He shook her hard and flung her back against the pillows. Connie lay there shocked and bewildered.

She could see a deep scratch on the side of his neck as he dressed for work and stormed out of the house.

Several times that day, she thought of calling Jane, but she knew what would happen. Jane would want her to leave, and she didn't have the courage to do that. There was no use dragging Jane into all of this. Things would work out.

Connie spent the day cleaning. She made a special dinner, but Matt didn't come home to eat. She ate alone and went to bed. She was still awake when he came in late, but she pretended to be asleep. She couldn't stand another quarrel tonight. She was as close to breaking as the threads in the lily pattern.

Before daybreak, Matt's cursing woke her. She thought he was angry with her, but he was talking to someone in the room.

"Matt, what's wrong?" she asked.

"Stop it!" he screamed. This time his voice held pain.

Connie turned on the light by the bed. Matt was striking at something beside the bed—something Connie couldn't see.

Matt continued to struggle and Connie heard something hit the floor. Matt stumbled from the bed, holding his pillow to his neck. Blood was streaming from a long, deep wound.

Connie looked over the side of the bed. A pair of scissors was on the floor.

"Get out!" Matt screamed, weaving toward the stairs. "Leave me alone."

"Matt, who are you talking to?" asked Connie.

Matt didn't answer. He staggered back to bed and fell backward on the pillow.

A soft laugh came from the stairs. Matt had been talking to that sound.

"I'll get rid of her, Connie," Matt whispered. "I did it once before."

"What are you talking about?" asked Connie. She had begun to cry.

"Lily," he said. "I know she's here."

"Oh, no! You killed Lily!" she cried, over and over.

Connie held her pillow and rocked back and forth.

There was someone in the room again. She felt a presence by the bed. She saw threads snapping all around her, as if they were being snipped by invisible scissors. Matt screamed and thrashed on the bed beside her. She wanted to help, but she felt herself snapping inside like the threads. She watched threads flying everywhere—long, strong threads—weaving, wrapping, cutting, until Matt lay lifeless.

The footsteps went back to the stairs and stopped. The long threads disappeared.

Connie watched the blood spread on the pillow.

"It looks like a lily pad," she thought.

She felt the giggles rising in her throat.

"Matt's gone and I'm in Lily's pad," she laughed.

She picked the pillow up and held it close. She knew she'd never get the stain out, but now it didn't matter. She wasn't ever going to get out of bed again. Lily was waiting for her in the hall, but she didn't care. Lily would be angry about the stain, so she would stay right here. Let Lily wait!

Connie giggled again. She hated confrontations.

Households

Emma Jones walked with dignity toward the kitchen door of the Austin country estate for the last time. Holding a potted plant with one hand and her scarred old suitcase with the other, she paused long enough to look directly into the eyes of Arlene Riggs, who sat at the table drinking coffee and looking very satisfied at Emma's departure.

"You win for now, Ms. Riggs," Emma said quietly. "I'm leaving, but you don't have as much of a hold on this house as you think you do. The battle's not over until the flowers are growing on your grave. One day you'll regret what you've done to me."

Arlene threw back her head with a throaty laugh.

"We'll see," she smirked.

Arlene quickly changed her smirk to a look of sympathy and concern as Maurice Austin came in the door. His shoulders sagged with disappointment.

"Emma, won't you please change your mind and stay?" he asked. "I can't imagine how I can get along without you."

"I can imagine," thought Arlene.

For some time now, Arlene had been picturing how this household could get along without Emma. Maurice would never marry as long as Emma ran his household so efficiently. She had to get Emma out of the way without making herself look bad.

She smiled slyly at Emma, but she was careful not to let Maurice see her.

Arlene had worked hard to make Emma feel like an outsider, and her subtle plan had succeeded. With Emma out of the way, Arlene could come over more often and do things for Maurice. Little by little, he would start to depend on her. Then she'd have a hold on him like the one Emma had had on this house for the past twenty-two years.

Emma stood looking at Maurice. The pain in her eyes was clear as she shook her head.

"No," she said. "It's better this way. This place has changed. You need your privacy and I need mine. Goodbye, Mr. Austin. Take care of yourself."

"What will you do, Emma?" he asked, even though they had been over this before.

"I have plans," she repeated, as she had several times earlier when they'd talked.

"At least let me drive you into town," Maurice offered.

"No, thank you," she answered. "The bus is coming soon."

"If you'll tell me where you're staying, I'll bring the rest of your flowers when I come to town," he told her.

"No, keep them. They belong here," she said, taking the potted plant she held in her hand and placing it on the shelf above the pantry door. "I always did think that flowers and plants brighten up a household."

The flowers and plants were so much a part of Emma's daily life that Maurice couldn't imagine her without them.

"Thank you, Emma," he said.

"You're welcome," she told him. "Maybe they'll make your life a little brighter."

"Somehow I'll get rid of those flowers," thought Arlene.

Maurice offered to carry Emma's suitcase when they saw the bus coming, but she shook her head and walked to the road alone, without looking back.

His eyes blurred with tears as he watched her pay the driver and take a seat. He felt very empty when the bus pulled away.

Emma had been his housekeeper ever since he and Jan had married twenty-two years ago. When Jan died, it was Emma who had kept the house running smoothly and held the family together until the children went away to school. He couldn't believe she was gone, and he still wasn't quite sure why she had left.

The trouble had started when he met Arlene. He'd never known Emma to dislike anyone as much as she disliked Arlene. Emma complained about having to clean up after Arlene when she came for a visit. As far as he could recall, it was the only real complaint Emma had made in all the years she'd worked for him. Finally, Emma had flatly refused to do anything if Arlene was in the house, and it was the only time that he and Emma had ever had words over her duties.

He thought Arlene had been very understanding about the whole matter. She had pointed out that Emma might be having a hard time adjusting to having another woman around the house after Jan's death. Emma had probably begun to feel that she was the lady of the house, and she might be experiencing a little jealousy.

Maurice wasn't sure he agreed, but she could be right. He was no expert on women.

After Emma's departure, Arlene left Maurice to his thoughts while she sat quietly at the table and recalled the groundwork she had so cunningly laid to force Emma to go. She should be happy now, but something was not quite right. When Emma had said, "You win, for now," Arlene had gotten the strangest feeling that it was a threat. She laughed nervously. What could Emma possibly do to her? She had already taken care of Emma! Now she had Maurice all to herself.

Poor, gullible Maurice! He hadn't understood why Emma was not grateful when Arlene popped in unexpectedly with a delicious meal and told Emma to freeze what she had cooked for another day. When she invited Emma to join them, Maurice believed that her invitation was sincere. Emma had seen through her, of course, but she didn't care. She had succeeded in making Emma feel that she wasn't needed and that she was an outsider who was only in the way. Arlene was sure of her success when Maurice reprimanded Emma about her duties. They had exchanged words, and Emma had hurried to her room, hurt and angry. The situation had become impossible for her. She had her pride. She knew she had to go.

Maurice had been truly shocked when Emma told him she was leaving. He tried to convince her that they could work out their problems, but she insisted that she could no longer stay. He apologized about the reprimand. He told her he knew she didn't like Arlene, but that they were only friends and that Arlene wouldn't be around that much.

Emma's decision was firm.

Maurice couldn't understand her attitude. Emma had said nothing about any of his other lady friends before Arlene. That was why he didn't think that Arlene was right about Emma being jealous. He had hoped that the three of them could sit down this weekend and work things out, but Emma had packed as soon as Arlene arrived. Now she was gone.

Maurice stood watching the bus until it was a tiny speck in the distance. He felt a soft hand on his arm, and he looked down to see Arlene in her smart business suit smiling up at him.

"Come inside," she said. "Let me fix you something to eat. You'll feel better."

He didn't think so, but he followed her inside. He was a little annoyed with himself for not handling the whole thing better, and the feeling was beginning to nag him. Arlene had a way of leading him around, and he was annoyed about that, too.

Right away, he began to feel guilty. Arlene had been wonderful to him. He should be grateful. She'd been a rock of support when Jan was ill. She had helped him straighten out his financial records, and he had appreciated the way she knew the value of a dollar. It was just that lately, she seemed to be getting a little too serious about their relationship. They were just friends. He wasn't ready for anything more than that. She told him she understood, but he was beginning to wonder.

"I can stay around and help you for a few days," Arlene offered after they'd eaten. "I could at least interview some housekeepers for you."

The guilt gave way to annoyance again. This was the kind of thing she had been doing—just taking over! This was one time when Arlene was not going to get her way. He insisted that he needed to have some time alone, and that she should go on home.

Arlene realized she was pushing too much, so she told him she understood. Maurice was relieved that she left without an argument.

He sat for a long time thinking that something must be wrong with him. He really admired Arlene. She'd gone through the ordeal of her husband's death and the ugly rumors that followed, and she hadn't sat around feeling sorry for herself.

He had never believed for a minute that she had given her husband the wrong medicine. Everyone knew that Arlene didn't have anything to do with dispensing medication at the hospital. She was assigned strictly to the records. She had certainly never made the slightest error on Jan's records or bills. She didn't have any more reason to kill her husband than she would have to—to kill his Jan!

It occurred to him that maybe Emma disliked Arlene because of those rumors.

He wished he knew where Emma was and what she was doing. He pictured her sitting alone in a tiny room, and it bothered him that she should be there when she could be here in this house, with the acres and acres of land that she loved around her. She was part of his family, and he missed her.

Maybe he should try to find her and bring her back. He decided against that. It would be better to give her a little time to think things over.

He looked at all the flowers and plants that Emma had left behind. He had an odd but comforting feeling when he looked at them. One by one, he carried them to the patio to give them some sun. He left the one on the shelf above the pantry. He couldn't bring himself to move it since Emma had put it there. She had placed it up there as if she had a special reason.

It was strange to be alone in the house. He finally went up to his own room.

While he was undressing for bed, the phone rang. He hoped to hear Emma's voice when he picked it up, but it was Arlene inviting him to dinner on Thursday. He heard himself agreeing to go.

When Thursday came, he wished that he had said no. He was tired and worried about Emma. He wanted to be home in case she called. He had tried all week to locate her, and he'd left messages for her all over town. He called his brother and told him he'd be at Arlene's, just in case Emma called there trying to get in touch.

Once he got to Arlene's, he enjoyed himself. She was a gourmet cook, and she had fixed everything that he especially liked. He was just finishing off a piece of apple pie when the phone interrupted. Arlene answered and handed it to him.

The color drained from Maurice's face as he listened. His brother had told the sheriff where Maurice would be.

Maurice put the receiver down and covered his face with his hands.

"Maurice, what is it?" Arlene asked.

His voice broke when he answered.

"It's Emma," he said. "They found her hanging in her room in a boarding house a few minutes ago."

The news shocked Arlene and left her a little frightened. She'd never expected this. She didn't know how it would affect Maurice.

Maurice could barely remember leaving. He was filled with grief as he drove into town. Arlene had offered to go along, but he had told her to stay at home. Emma wouldn't have wanted her there.

After Maurice left, Arlene sat reviewing her tactics. Maurice would feel guilty about Emma's death and begin to withdraw. She couldn't let that happen. If she left him alone too long, he might get to like it. She'd have to be more subtle, but she had to make her move now.

A wonderful idea came to her. She'd start by just being a friend again. She'd drive out and have a hot, delicious snack waiting for him when he got home that night. He wouldn't want to be alone after seeing Emma that way. She would encourage him to talk, and he'd soon realize how much he needed her.

She decided to surprise him completely by hiding her car in the shed around back. She went in the door by the patio. Maurice never kept it locked. She needed to fix the food right away for their snack, for he'd probably be getting home soon.

First, she'd need to check the pantry to see what he had on hand. She opened the pantry door and stood looking at the rows of jars, many of which Emma had filled with vegetables from the garden the summer before.

A quick movement under the lowest shelf caught Arlene's attention. A little field mouse blinked up at her and then scurried as fast as it could go through a hole in the pantry wall.

Arlene gasped and then laughed. Her laugh sounded loud because the house was so silent.

"It's too quiet," she thought. "I wish Maurice would come home."

The shelf above the pantry door creaked ever so slightly, and something started to slide. Arlene looked up just as Emma's potted plant came crashing down, striking her in the face. The blow sent her reeling back against the shelves. She bounced off the sharp edges and slid to the floor, surprised and stunned. As her head struck the bottom shelf, the pantry door slammed shut. She tried to wipe away the broken bits of the plant and clay pot that covered her, but she couldn't move.

She said a silent prayer of thanks as she heard Maurice's car pull into the garage. She tried to call out when she heard him come through the door, but she couldn't speak.

She heard him dial the phone. He put it down and dialed again. He was probably calling her. No, now he was talking to his brother. She wanted to call out again, but she was bleeding from the cuts and she was feeling weak. She'd save her strength until he got off the phone.

She made an effort to concentrate, but the blackness came and went. She must have missed part of what he was saying. She heard "airport ... back in two days ... Emma's funeral in her hometown." Oh, no! He couldn't be going away! He couldn't!

Maurice crossed to the bedroom. She knew he'd be packing. He packed fast. She had to make some kind of noise to get him to notice, but she blacked out again. He came from the bedroom and went to the door. She had to make him hear her. It was her only chance. Nobody knew she was here! She summoned all her strength.

"Mur...." she gurgled, trying to call his name.

The sound was too faint. The door clicked shut, and Arlene heard the car drive away.

She opened her eyes and the inky blackness turned to shadows. One swayed back and forth—first it was a woman, then it was a noose that was empty. She must be hallucinating. She closed her eyes and then opened them again. The shadows were gone, but the walls were closing in, holding her prisoner in the empty house.

Her head rolled to one side and her body shuddered once.

The little field mouse poked its head through the hole in the wall, twitched its tiny nose, and fled from the smell of death.

The roots of the broken plant in the pantry kept their hold on the soil in the shattered pot.

In the kitchen, a shadow moved along the wall and out to the patio. It stopped by the pots that Maurice had carried there. Everything was growing in the sun. Emma Jones's flowers had never looked brighter and greener.

The Handle

When Ernie Meyers heard the clunking sound against his window, he knew he was in for the biggest trouble of his life. He didn't need to look out. He knew what it was and who was throwing it. He even knew why. He hadn't dared to tell anyone at first. Now he didn't know what to do. He wished somebody else knew what was happening.

He knew that his mother suspected that something awful was troubling him. She had even backed off from scolding him about the condition of his room last Saturday. She had come to call him to dinner, and she noticed the dirty old handle in the middle of the floor in front of his dresser.

"Ernie, what on earth is this?" she asked.

"Just a handle, Mom," Ernie answered, looking up from his baseball cards.

"I can see that," she said impatiently. "But where did it come from and what's it doing here?"

"You don't want to know, Mom," thought Ernie. "Believe me, you don't want to know."

Aloud he said, "Just something of Jason's."

"I'm sorry, honey," she said.

Ernie looked from his mother back to his baseball cards and put the one he'd gotten from Jason under the stack.

Ernie had actually been pretending that the handle wasn't there. He'd seen it on the floor when he first woke up, but he didn't want to touch it. All day he had walked around it. It upset him to see it there.

He was glad his mother didn't pursue the matter, even though she must have sensed his uneasiness. She just reached down, picked up the handle, and placed it on the windowsill. A cool breeze blew, billowing out the curtains, making them look like ghosts. The handle toppled off the sill and fell to the ground, startling Ernie's mother. She wanted to ask Ernie more about the handle, but she decided the time was not right. Instead, she smiled at Ernie.

"Come to dinner," she said.

She waited while Ernie put his cards away and joined her. The curtains were still billowing out at him when they left the room.

Ernie would have liked to believe that he would never see the handle again, but he knew he would. He wished he could tell his parents what was happening, but he didn't know how they could help. Nobody could help him now. All he could do was wait.

After dinner, he went into the living room to watch TV. He didn't feel brave enough to go back to his room just yet. He could hear his parents in the dining room, talking about him and the handle. They didn't know the significance of the handle, but they were worried about him. They blamed his moody behavior on the shock of the accident that had killed his best friend, Jason York.

He was indeed thinking about his friend's death, but he wasn't missing him. He couldn't tell his parents, because they wouldn't understand, but he wasn't missing Jason because Jason was back!

Jason's funeral had been on a Sunday. But on Monday morning, Ernie had seen him on the corner at the bus stop, one block from school. Ernie had run to meet him at first, just as he always had—forgetting that Jason was dead! As Ernie got close, Jason vanished. Ernie couldn't find a trace of him, except for the handle.

Ernie knew at once what it was. It belonged to Jason. Ernie ought to know. He had stared at it long enough after Jason died.

Ernie ran from the corner, leaving the handle on the sidewalk. He was breathless when he reached school, and he barely had time to open his locker before the bell.

As he reached in and grabbed his science book, something slid out and hit the floor. It was the handle. It couldn't be—he'd left it on the sidewalk minutes ago. Yet there it was. Ernie felt a cool breeze on the back of his neck, and he glanced over his shoulder. There stood Jason, looking just as he had looked on the last day he was alive. Ernie blinked, and the vision was gone.

He wanted to tell Jason that he was sorry, but how could you talk to someone who was dead?

That was the last time Ernie went anywhere alone. As long as he was with other students, he hadn't seen Jason appear. He was beginning to feel safe. Then last Saturday, the handle had turned up in his room.

After the handle fell out, Ernie slept with his window closed. Tonight he had heard the clunk against the window, and he knew the time he'd been dreading had come. Jason was back!

Ernie didn't stir, but the clunking continued until the panes in the window rattled. He couldn't stand it. He had to see. He barely pulled the curtains open and peeked through. Just as he suspected, Jason was out there.

"Jason, I'm sorry," Ernie whispered. "I'm sorry about the quarrel and the stupid baseball card. I'm sorry I did what I did. Go away, Jason. Please go away and leave me alone!"

Jason didn't move.

Ernie began to shake with silent sobs. He thought about the last time he and Jason had been together. They had argued, but they had called a truce. Ernie had given Jason a ride home from school on the handlebars of his bicycle. All was going well until Jason laughed at the way he had outsmarted Ernie and gotten the one baseball card Ernie really wanted. Anger welled up in Ernie all over again. Jason didn't notice. He waved the card in the air and kept laughing at Ernie.

Ernie didn't plan what happened. He jerked the handlebars, intending to dump Jason in the street. A truck came speeding out of nowhere at the same instant, and Jason went flying under the wheels. Out of all the confusion that followed, Ernie remembered only one thing clearly. Jason's baseball card was on the pavement, face up by the curb. Ernie reached down and put it in his pocket.

He'd been sorry ever since, and now Jason was going to make him pay.

Ernie could still see Jason standing in the yard, watching the window. He ran to his desk, grabbed the card, and held it up for Jason to see.

"Here! You can have it back," said Ernie.

Jason reached down and picked up the handle that had bounced back from the window when he'd thrown it earlier. He threw it again, this time with such force that it crashed though the glass. Ernie felt slivers from the panes slice his skin as they showered around him.

Ernie dropped the card through the broken window. Jason made no move to pick it up. The card wasn't what he wanted. He raised his hand and motioned for Ernie to come out.

"No! I won't go with you!" screamed Ernie.

He grabbed up the dirt-covered handle and shook it at the ghostly figure below.

Jason motioned again.

"Leave me alone," shrieked Ernie. "Get out of here!"

Ernie's parents burst into the room. They looked, wild-eyed, at the broken window and their hysterical son.

"What's going on here?" asked his father.

Ernie couldn't answer. His father shook him gently.

"Tell me!" he insisted.

"Make him go away!" cried Ernie. "I gave him the card, but he doesn't want it now. He wants to take me with him."

"What are you talking about?" asked his mother.

"I killed Jason!" he told her. "I didn't mean to. He's out there now. He's come back to get me! I don't want to go with him. I don't want to die!"

His mother put her arms around him.

"Shhh," she said. "You are going to be all right."

His father crossed to the window and looked out. The yard was empty.

"Whoever it was is gone now," he said.

His mother led him to his bed, but he still stood sobbing and clutching the handle.

"What are you holding?" asked his mother. "Isn't that the same handle I saw in your room last week?"

Ernie stopped crying and nodded.

"Let me see it," said his father.

"It's Jason's," said Ernie. "He's brought it to me."

"That's impossible," said his father. "Jason's dead. Where did this come from?"

Ernie didn't answer, because footsteps were coming toward the door. The doorknob turned, and the three stared as the door opened. Jason York stood in the doorway, and the stench of death filled the room.

Ernie sank to the floor, and the handle dropped from his hand and lay still.

His father knelt beside him.

"He's fainted," said his father. "He'll be all right."

"No," Ernie whispered, struggling to make them hear. "The handle..."

They leaned closer because his voice was fading.

"The handle is Jason's," he said. "I saw it the day of the funeral. It's the handle from his coffin."

Ernie stopped speaking and closed his eyes. His parents held each other and cried.

A cool breeze blew through the broken window, dislodging particles of dirt from the handle and blowing them across the face of the dead boy.

The Whittler

Arnold Fremont finished the scary tale and watched the last piece of wood turn to ashes in the campfire. It left him with an empty feeling. He had decided this would be his last year to come here. He was beginning to feel all the terror he had felt ten years ago.

"Time for bed," he told the boys.

"Just one more story, please!" they begged.

"Tell us 'The Whittler'," said Dwayne Kelsey.

Dwayne had been on the camping trip the year before when Arnold had told the story. Dwayne had liked it so much that he had sneaked out of camp that night and gone down the road to the old graveyard, to see the whittler's grave. Arnold had warned Dwayne that if he pulled anything like that again this year, he'd never bring him on a church trip again.

It hadn't been hard to get Dwayne to promise. Dwayne had been one frightened little boy that night when he had come running back to camp. He had sworn that the whittler was following him.

Arnold knew that wasn't true, but he knew *someone* had been after Dwayne that night.

After Arnold had gotten Dwayne settled down and back in bed that night, he had taken a look around. He had found shavings strewn along the path. That's when he had felt the terror and had known that somebody had been there that night. He told Dwayne that it had probably been an animal following him. He tried to believe that himself. He didn't know what he'd do if he came face to face with the whittler.

After that night excursion, Dwayne had certainly gained prestige with the other boys. Anyone brave enough to go alone to the grave of the whittler in the middle of the night was an unqualified hero in their eyes. The respect he gained from being chased by this apparition had lasted beyond camp, all through the school year.

"Please tell us about the whittler," the boys pleaded.

Arnold thought about the events that had taken place, and hesitated. He suspected that Dwayne only wanted to relive last year's glory, and retelling the story could give some of the other boys the idea to try it.

"Please!" the boys urged him.

"Well, all right," Arnold agreed. "But if anybody pulls a stunt like Dwayne did last year, we'll go home in the morning and I'll never take you camping again! Understand?"

"Yes, Mr. Fremont," they chorused.

Arnold poked at the coals and cleared his throat. Only a few coals glowed in the dark, like eyes. The wiggly bodies became still and every face, barely visible in the pale light of the dying fire, turned toward Arnold.

"The whittler was a man named Aaron Upton," Arnold began. "He used to live right down the road from here. He was always whittling on a piece of wood, all the time."

"Did you ever see him?" asked little Drew Webster from the back of the circle.

"Yes," said Arnold. "The day he was hanged. I was a young man ten years ago. I had just come here."

Arnold sat staring into the darkness beyond the camp until Drew spoke again and brought him back from his thoughts.

"What was he like?" the boy wanted to know.

"People said he was fascinating to watch," said Arnold. "He could carve anything he wanted to. He could have been a great artist, but that wasn't his ambition. He liked to keep to himself as much as he could. He'd stand and whittle on a piece of wood until there was nothing but a pile of shavings, or he'd make a perfect likeness of an animal for some child who happened by. He just did whatever caught his fancy. Nobody could handle a knife the way he could. That special ability of his was what made people think he did the killing."

"Who did he kill?" they asked.

"Why did he do it?"

"Is that why he was hanged?"

Arnold poked the coals again and added a small piece of wood before he answered.

"He killed a little boy about your age, they said. The boy was cut to pieces. It was an awful thing."

"Why did they think Aaron Upton did it just because he whittled?" asked Dwayne. "Cutting up a kid is not like cutting up a piece of wood."

"Maybe it was because he was a loner," said Arnold. "If you keep to yourself, people get funny ideas."

He remembered how he'd joined the church soon after he came to town, right after what he had seen happen to Aaron Upton. He didn't want anybody getting ideas about him.

"Everybody was up in arms," Arnold continued. "People were afraid to go out at night. They couldn't come up with a motive or a murder weapon. Aaron was the only one they knew who was handy with a knife. They convinced themselves that he was guilty. They figured he'd buried the knife someplace in these woods after the killing. They got so worked up, they didn't wait for a trial. A mob just went out and lynched him. The old oak tree he died on is still standing right here in these woods."

The boys inched closer together.

"Are you sure you want to hear the rest of this story?" asked Arnold.

"Yes!" they assured him.

"I wasn't one of the mob—I had just come here—but I watched the hanging. I was just a young man. Now look at me. I have grown old in ten years because of that killing. I look twice my age."

"Didn't he tell them that he was innocent?" asked Drew.

"Oh, yes," said Arnold. "He faced his accusers and told them he didn't do it. He even looked at me. I turned away—I couldn't help him. They buried him in the old graveyard down the road."

The boys began to speak at once again.

"I wonder if he really did it!"

"I'd be afraid to come back if I had been there when he died."

"I have been afraid," admitted Arnold. "I have felt like running many times. But what if something terrible happened in the next place I went? I've stayed here because I know that it's really a safe place to be."

The boys didn't look so sure. Arnold couldn't let them know that their instincts were right. He'd felt things building up for a long time. He was afraid something horrible was going to happen again very soon. That's why he had decided not to come back with the boys again after this outing.

Arnold wished that he hadn't started the story tonight. All those feelings he'd bottled up began to boil inside. He knew now that he needed to end the story quickly and get the boys to bed.

"It wasn't long after the hanging," he told them, "that the sheriff got a report that the little boy had been seen getting into a strange car the day he was killed. The new evidence pointed to the fact that they had punished the wrong man."

"What happened then?" they wanted to know.

"People felt guilty, and they began going to Aaron's grave. Some went to pray; some went to put flowers on it. Old Aaron didn't seem to be a forgiving soul. When they disturbed him, he climbed out of his grave and followed them home, leaving a trail of shavings along the way."

"Did he really follow you last year, Dwayne?"

The question came from a little boy next to Arnold Fremont.

"He sure did!" said Dwayne. "There were shavings all around my sleeping bag. There were even some by yours, too. Right, Mr. Fremont?"

"Well, yes," said Arnold, "but..."

The boys now gave Dwayne their full attention.

"I'd sure like to see the grave and the oak tree," said Drew. "Would you be scared to go back, Dwayne?"

Arnold was surprised by his answer.

"Yeah," he told the boys, "I think I would be scared. But not because of the whittler. Something happened that night that I never told anyone about. There was more than one thing after me that night. I think one was the whittler's ghost, but I think the other one was human. I know this sounds crazy, but I think the whittler wanted to protect me from the human!"

Dwayne's statement made everyone, including Arnold, uneasy. Nobody objected when Arnold told them it was time to go to bed.

Arnold continued to sit by the fire until he was sure it was out. Dwayne's revelation about a live person being out there left Arnold shaken. He'd have to pursue the matter with Dwayne when he caught him alone. There was no reason to bother the other boys.

For the first time in years, Arnold checked his pocket to make sure he had his knife. In view of Dwayne's news, he might be forced to use it.

After he checked his knife, he checked on the boys. The first day in camp had worn them out. They were already asleep.

Arnold crawled into his own sleeping bag, but he was wide awake. The moon was full and bright, and as he lay looking up at it, all the old restless feelings came back.

Arnold remembered what it had been like growing up in an orphanage. One by one, he'd watched other little boys get adopted. He'd dreamed of the places he'd go and the things he'd do if he ever got out of there. He'd made a place for himself here, but at times, he still felt like that little unwanted boy again.

He remembered the night he had left the orphanage for good. He had barely turned twenty. He had hitched a ride, and the man even let him drive the car. When they got a room for the night, he had waited until the man was asleep and then had taken the car for a short drive. He'd had it back before the man woke up.

Of course, there was that ugly business about the murder of the little boy. He had stayed on because he didn't want to make people think he had anything to hide.

The last ten years had not been all bad. He had made progress and had worked well with these boys. Dwayne was the only one who had caused him a problem, but he could handle that.

Arnold was beginning to get sleepy. There was no reason for him to stay awake. There was nothing out there. Or was there? He heard a snap, a sound like someone stepping on a twig. He listened intently. He was right. Someone was walking. Surely Dwayne hadn't disobeyed him again!

He crawled out of his sleeping bag and walked toward the slumbering boys. One of them must be up, playing a joke on him. He heard more twigs snapping and he felt in his pocket for his knife.

"Joke's over, boys!" he called. "Come on out!"

The boys sat up in their sleeping bags, rubbing their eyes and asking what was going on.

Arnold was getting angry. He should have dealt with Dwayne last year when he had the chance. Now he had everybody in camp up.

Arnold could hear footsteps now, coming down the trail that led from the graveyard to the camp. He could see someone approaching through the shadows.

"Dwayne Kelsey, I want to see you!" shouted Arnold.

"Yes, sir, Mr. Fremont," said Dwayne, his voice coming from among the other boys.

He whirled around. If Dwayne was with the other boys, then who was coming down the trail?

The footsteps stopped, and Arnold could see that the boys were staring, spellbound, at the figure standing behind him.

"The whittler!" he heard Drew gasp. "But why is he pointing at you, Mr. Fremont?"

Arnold turned around again slowly, for he knew that Drew was right.

Arnold took his knife from his pocket. He advanced toward the dark form waiting in the shadows.

"I'm sorry," he said. "I couldn't tell them I did it. I've made up for it. I've helped these boys. I wouldn't hurt any of them—not even Dwayne. I was going to leave after this trip."

The dark figure remained motionless, still pointing his finger.

Arnold stopped and bowed his head for an instant. Then with a sudden gesture, he turned the knife toward himself and plunged it into his heart. Warm, fresh blood covered the old, dried stains on the knife from ten years earlier.

The boys didn't move until the dark figure retraced its steps to the graveyard. Then they looked at Arnold. His face was covered with a layer of shavings from the wood of the old oak that they knew as the hanging tree.

Where Freddy Is

"Nobody knows where Freddy is," little Alma Travers reported to her mother. "I went as far as Mrs. Bailey's, and nobody has seen him."

Ruby Travers looked down at her daughter and wished that Freddy could be more like his sister. She never wandered off and gave them trouble.

"Asa," she called to her husband, who was plowing the garden. "Freddy's took off again. I don't believe that boy's brain and feet are connected. He just walks off without thinking to tell anybody."

"He's probably just walking in the woods again," Asa called back. "You know he likes to explore new places."

"You'd think he'd have enough exploring to do in a new house! If he's not back in a few minutes, I want you to go and look for him," she said.

Asa nodded and continued plowing, and Ruby went back inside the house.

Freddy was exactly where his father thought he was. He was walking down a cool, shady path deep in the woods.

Freddy wanted to keep walking, but his stomach was beginning to remind him that it was lunch time. He knew his mother would be upset with him for going off without telling her. He wished he could find something to take to her as a peace offering.

He stopped and surveyed his immediate surroundings. Then he saw the very thing he needed by the path right in front of him. It was the brightest red flower he had ever seen. She loved flowers. This would make her forget how worried she had been. He picked it up and ran down the path toward home.

When he reached his house, he proudly handed the red flower to his mother. That, and the relief she felt at seeing him safe, delayed her lecture until after lunch. When he asked to go back outside to play, she sat him down for a talk.

"I don't want you going off alone," she told him. "We don't know what might be out there in the woods. You could get hurt or lost. Promise me that you'll stay in the yard."

Freddy promised, and he kept his promise for the rest of that day. The next morning was a different story.

Freddy went outside right after breakfast. He was watching a bee buzzing around a delicate white flower, when a beautiful yellow butterfly flew right by him and disappeared into the woods. The next thing he knew, his feet had carried him back into the woods again. His presence scared a little brown rabbit, and it raced off through the underbrush. Freddy left the familiar path and gave chase. Soon the rabbit was gone, and Freddy was lost.

Freddy had never been lost before, and he didn't know what he should do. Nobody would come looking for him, because nobody knew where he was. He picked a direction and started walking.

He hadn't gone far when he came to a clearing with a neat little house built in the middle. Beside the front porch was a rosebush like one he had seen only in a seed catalog, and it was full of blue roses! His mother would surely forgive him for breaking his promise if he took her something so beautiful!

He dashed across the yard and broke off a big, blue rose. As he turned to go, the door opened and an old woman emerged, shaking a broom at him.

"Get away from my roses! Get away!" she shouted, coming down the steps and following him as he hurried across the yard.

Freddy thought she'd stop at the path, but she kept following him, yelling and waving her broom.

"She's a witch!" thought Freddy, remembering his mother's warning that they didn't know what might be in the woods.

He began to run as fast as he could, looking back just once to see if the old lady was following him. He saw her clutch her heart and sink down to the ground beside the path.

He started to go back, but she yelled again, "If I catch you bothering my roses again, I'll put you where nobody will ever find you!"

Freddy believed her. He hesitated only a second and then continued to run. His feet led him to a path that curved to the left of a big birch tree,and then Freddy recognized the place where he usually played. He slowed his pace, but didn't stop completely until he was in is own yard again.

Freddy knew he was in trouble when he saw his father, mother, sister, and Mrs. Bailey from down the road all gathered in the yard.

"Where have you been, young man?" his mother demanded to know. "We've been looking everywhere for you!"

"I found a witch's house," explained Freddy, "and she chased me when I picked this beautiful blue rose for you."

Freddy held out the rose like an offering to his mother. The scowl on her face softened, but she suppressed the smile that started.

"Freddy," she said sternly, "what am I going to do with you? You know you are not suppose to go into other people's yards and pick their flowers."

"It was a witch's house," Freddy repeated.

Mrs. Bailey began to laugh.

"You've been to Phoebe Ashburn's place," she said. "She's no witch, but she's a strange one! And she's the only one in the county that grows blue roses."

"But she chased me with a broom," said Freddy. "She even threatened to catch me and put me where nobody would ever find me if I ever bother her roses again."

Little Alma looked frightened.

"Do you think she could do that?" she asked.

"Poor old Phoebe couldn't catch much of anything," said Mrs. Bailey. "She has a heart condition."

"Oh, no!" said Freddy. Then he told them how he'd left her lying by the path.

"Go inside and stay with your sister," said Asa. "Don't come outside until we get back."

Mrs. Bailey led Ruby and Asa to Phoebe Ashburn's cottage. She was still lying by the path when they found her, but she was dead. The strain of running had been too much for her heart.

Freddy felt terrible about the whole thing, but he told himself it wasn't his fault. He hadn't forced her to run. He hadn't known she had a bad heart.

Among her papers, Phoebe Ashburn had left a request that her blue rosebush be planted by her grave. Those in charge were reluctant to carry out her wishes, because they felt sure that transplanting the bush would cause it to die. But in the end, they felt obligated to grant her final request, so they placed the blue rosebush by her headstone. Much to their surprise, it thrived.

For several days after Phoebe Ashburn's funeral, Freddy moped around feeling bored. His parents had strictly forbidden him to go out of the yard, so he had nothing to do but think about what had happened.

What was the big deal about one rose anyway? They couldn't be that hard to grow. He could probably do it himself. Maybe he'd go down to the graveyard after supper and get a cutting and plant it under his window. If his mother had her own blue roses, maybe she wouldn't be so mad at him.

Ruby Travers had finished the supper dishes when she realized she hadn't seen Freddy since he left the table. She looked out in the yard and he was not there. She checked his room, but Alma said he hadn't been there, either.

"Asa!" Ruby called. "I don't know where Freddy is!"

Asa checked the barn and the path leading to the woods. There was no sign of Freddy. Then Asa noticed his son's tracks heading down the road toward the graveyard.

Asa's stomach knotted. He told himself to relax. Freddy had wandered away dozens of times and he was always fine. But Asa couldn't convince himself this time that Freddy was all right. He felt that it was urgent for him to go to the graveyard.

When Ruby and Alma saw Asa hurrying down the road, they quickly followed. They could see Freddy's tracks quite clearly in the dirt. They led up to Phoebe Ashburn's grave and stopped.

They had no idea why Freddy would come here.

Asa stood with his wife and daughter, staring at the cracked earth above Phoebe's grave. The blue rosebush beside the headstone was broken over.

"Where do you suppose he is?" Ruby asked her husband.

"Do you think old Phoebe Ashburn got him like she said she would?" asked Alma.

"I'm sure he's around here somewhere," said Asa, but he was becoming more and more concerned.

Alma walked around Phoebe's grave examining the ground.

"Look," she said. "Freddy's tracks are headed back for the house."

Ruby and Asa looked where she was pointing. The tracks did indeed head away, evenly spaced. Asa told himself this was a good sign. Ruby relaxed a little.

They followed the tracks, and then saw that the spaces became wider and the tracks deeper, as if Freddy had started to run.

Alma ran ahead of her parents.

"There are Freddy's shoes!" she exclaimed.

"Why would he leave his shoes?" asked Ruby.

Alma had reached the shoes and picked them up.

"They're heavy!" she said, lifting them high in the air. "Something's inside."

"Let me see what it is," said Asa.

Ruby and Asa watched as Alma held one shoe in each hand. Their wildest nightmares could not have prepared them for what they saw. Before they could reach her, she turned the shoes over—and Freddy's feet fell out!

Mrs. Bailey heard the screaming and came running first. Then others came. They searched and searched, but came up empty-handed. Freddy's feet were all they ever found.

Beneath the window of Freddy's vacant room, a tiny blue rosebush pushed its way through the hard earth and began to grow. Nobody knows how it got there, and to this day, nobody has solved the mystery of where Freddy is.

Whispers

Wisshh!

Kim whirled around and looked at the rack of earrings behind her in the little shop. The weird sound had come from the rack, but there was only silence now. Kim saw one pair of earrings swaying ever so slightly, but she still couldn't tell where the sound had come from.

Wisshh!

She heard it again. She was watching, so this time it was obvious. The swaying earrings had made the noise. She couldn't look away. There was something hypnotic about the earrings.

"Mom! Dad!" Kim called to her parents, who were in front of the store by the counter. "These are what I want!"

"What have you found?" asked her mother as they came down the cluttered aisle and stopped next to the rack.

"These!" Kim repeated.

She reached over and touched the earrings. A tingle ran through her fingers.

"I wish I had these," she said. "They're perfect."

Kim's mother took one look and shook her head.

"I'm sorry, honey," she said, "but these are just not right for you."

"Why not?" Kim pouted. "I like them."

"They look like little leather tongues," said her mother.

Kim could see that her mother's mind was made up. Turning to her father, she gave him the smile that always got her whatever she wanted.

"Please, Daddy," she said. "It's my birthday. Can't I have them, please?"

Her father looked helplessly at her mother.

"Ruth," he said, "I really don't see anything wrong with the earrings. What's the harm in her having them?"

"Charles," her mother objected, "you always spoil her! The harm is that you never back me up. These things are revolting! They are not the style for a little girl of ten."

"It's her birthday. Can't we let her choose what she wants this once?" Charles pleaded.

Kim was already smiling smugly to herself. She knew the earrings were hers. Somehow she always managed to get everything she wished for.

Riding home with the package in her hand, Kim tried to change her mother's mind about the earrings. It wouldn't hurt to soften her up a little. It would be just like her mother to refuse to let her wear them to school. She *had* to wear them there. She knew she should from the time they whispered to her from the rack.

She wanted Becky Simon to see them. She didn't know why, but she felt the earrings would upset Becky Simon. And how Kim enjoyed upsetting Becky Simon!

"My friends will love my earrings," Kim told her mother.

"They may say that to your face," said her mother, "but they will whisper behind your back that you have poor taste."

"That's funny, Mom," laughed Kim. "You said my earrings look like little tongues, and now you say I have no taste!"

Kim's mother was not amused, so Kim decided to be quiet and let her mother get used to them little by little.

Kim usually put new earrings in her jewelry box, but when she went to bed that night, she put them on the nightstand by her bed. As she turned out the light, the same sound she'd heard in the store came like a whisper.

Wisshh!

Kim reached over and picked up the earrings. The moonlight shining through her window made them glow an eerie pink. Her fingers tingled again.

"It sounded like you just said 'wish,'" she said softly. "It sounded like that in the store, too. I wished for you and I got you. I wonder if I could wish for something else. Let's see. What would I like? I know! I wish I didn't have to go to school tomorrow."

Kim smiled as she laid the earrings back on the nightstand and snuggled down to sleep.

When Kim woke the next morning, she was burning with fever. Her mother took her temperature, called the doctor, and then phoned the school to say Kim would be absent. All day Kim tossed and turned, her whole body feeling like it was on fire. Then, just as quickly as it had come, the fever left. It was at the exact time that school ended. Nothing like that had ever happened to her before.

She was able to eat some soup for dinner and watch TV later. By bedtime, she was her normal self.

She looked at the earrings on the nightstand and wondered about the wish she had made the night before. Of course, earrings couldn't grant wishes, but it was odd how it had worked out.

She reached to turn off the light, when she heard the now-familiar sound.

Wisshh!

She picked up the earrings again and examined them closely. There was a faint pink glow about them again. This time, little spurts of energy shot through her hands. She nearly dropped the earrings. She thought about what she'd tell the girls about them at school the next day.

All the girls would be impressed except Becky Simon. Becky had all kinds of things, but even Becky didn't have anything like these earrings. Kim hated the way Becky was always showing off.

Kim had meant to take the earrings to school today, but she'd made that silly wish that had somehow come true. She wouldn't wish that again. There must be something she could wish for, though, to see if the earrings really granted wishes. Then she thought of the very thing that would give her a great deal of satisfaction.

"I wish," said Kim, holding the earrings close, "that I will make Becky Simon cry tomorrow!"

The next morning as she left for school, Kim slipped the earrings in her pocket. There was no use taking a chance on her mother seeing them and making her leave them at home.

On the way to school, Kim passed the little store where her father had bought the earrings. She looked at the sign, EXOTIC IMPORTS, and wondered where her earrings had originally come from. On an impulse, she went inside. It wouldn't hurt to ask. She might get an answer that would make a good story to tell the girls.

The salesman remembered her.

"How do you like your new earrings?" he asked.

"Oh, fine," said Kim. "I was just wondering if you could tell me where they came from."

"Well," he said, "I have so many items, I can't usually keep up with things like that, but I do remember that the pair your father bought for you came from Germany. They were handmade by a man who once had a little shop near one of the concentration camps in World War II. Some people say that his jewelry was actually made from parts of human bodies from the camp, but I never really believed that."

Kim didn't find the answer to her question as appealing as she had hoped it would be. She'd wanted it to be romantic instead of gruesome. Her stomach began to feel queasy and she backed out the door, mumbling something about being late for school.

By the time she got to school, she had recovered somewhat from the revulsion of the salesman's story. In fact, the more she thought about it, the more she thought she would use the story to shock the girls when she showed them the earrings. It would really freak out Becky Simon. Her grandmother had died in one of those concentration camps!

Becky was always talking about her grandmother and wishing she could have known her. She had once said to Kim that if her grandmother were alive, she wouldn't let anybody pick on her. This story about the earrings would probably make Becky cry!

Because of her visit to the shop, Kim was barely on time for class. She had no time to talk to anyone.

At lunch, she joined the girls on the sidewalk near the curb. She sat down and pulled the earrings from her pocket.

"See what I got for my birthday?" asked Kim. "There's not another pair like them anywhere."

The girls stared at the earrings with interest. Only Becky Simon remained aloof.

"They were made from parts of real humans in a concentration camp in Germany and they have special power," Kim continued. "These are made from tongues, and they can talk and grant wishes."

"That's the biggest lie I ever heard," said Becky Simon. "What kind of power can old earrings have?"

Kim was expecting the girls to believe her, so she was not prepared when they agreed with Becky.

"You're making that up," they said.

"I'm telling the truth!" Kim insisted.

"Prove it!" Becky dared her. "Wish for something right now."

Kim squeezed the earrings and felt the energy flowing through her.

Wisshh!

The sound came right on cue.

"There! Did you hear that?" Kim asked, holding out the earrings.

"Yes," said the girls. They had heard something.

"You haven't proven anything," said Becky. "You didn't make a wish. Nobody cares about your ugly old earrings."

"You're just jealous!" declared Kim.

"I am not," said Becky. "I think they're disgusting, and I think you're a liar!"

"These are probably made out of your grandmother's tongue," Kim shouted.

Becky's face turned red. She reached out and shoved Kim's shoulder. Kim was so angry, her knuckles were white from squeezing the earrings. She didn't think about what she was saying. Words just flew out of her mouth, as she struck at Becky with her free hand.

"You're so hateful, I wish I'd never see you again, Becky Simon!"

Becky's hand went up, blocking Kim's arm in midair. The jolt caused the earrings to go flying from Kim's hand. Kim grabbed for them, but they clinked through the grate over the sewer in the street.

Nobody moved.

Wisshh!

The sound came soft as a whisper as the earrings splashed into the water below.

Too late, Kim realized what she had done. This couldn't be happening. She had to change the wish!

"No!" she screamed, as she began to grope wildly on the grating. But she knew it was no use. The earrings were lost, but her last wish was granted. Tears were rolling down Becky Simon's face, but Kim couldn't see them. Kim's eyes were already beginning to blur, and Becky and the others were fading away in the darkness.

The Closet

Brian Alvey hated bedtime. When his mother tucked him in at night, Brian would beg her to push the closet door all the way shut. She would try, but she never quite got it closed.

"The door is warped, honey," she explained. "We'll have it repaired as soon as we can."

This promise did not satisfy Brian. With all the repairs they were already doing on this house, Brian knew it would be a long time before they got around to his closet door. If they didn't fix it soon, it would be too late. Something very dangerous was in that closet. He tried to convince his mother, but she didn't understand. Just because she couldn't see it didn't mean it wasn't there.

"There's nothing in the closet but your clothes and toys," she told him over and over.

Brian knew better. He had known since the first night he'd slept in his new room.

First, he'd heard the floorboards creaking inside the closet. He'd been too scared to look that night, but the next day he had stepped inside and tried to make them creak. They didn't make a sound for him, so whatever was in the closet must have been bigger than he was!

The next night, along with the creaking, Brian heard something crawling around on the floor. He didn't look, but he could feel several eyes watching him through the slightly open door. He knew that anytime they wanted to, they could creep out and get him.

The remodeling was coming along fairly well, but Brian's closet door was far down on the list of repairs.

Each night, Brian would lie in bed and listen to the things creeping and crawling around in his closet. He began to think of them as Creepy Crawlies. He would remember his old room in the other house where they'd lived, and he wished he could live there again. He knew it was impossible, though. His father's new job was in this town.

"Do you think he'll ever like this place?" Mrs. Alvey asked her husband one evening.

"Sure," he told her. "He just needs a little time to adjust."

Brian tried to explain that it wasn't the place that he didn't like; it was the Creepy Crawlies. He not only complained about the occupants of the closet now; he had begun to see them in his dreams, and every night he woke up screaming.

"Tell us about the dreams," his mother urged, but Brian couldn't remember the details clearly.

"They come through tunnels and they want out!" he said. "They look like shadows at first, but then they turn into horrible-looking people and start to crawl toward me!"

His parents had never seen Brian so upset. Nothing they said convinced him that he was safe, so fixing the closet door became a top priority in the Alvey household.

Brian felt a little better when the door was repaired and he could lock it. He could still hear the Creepy Crawlies, but now they couldn't stare at him through the open door.

What bothered him most now was that no one believed the Creepy Crawlies really existed. The door was holding them back for the present, but he worried that they might find a way to get out. He wished that somebody could see them or at least find some evidence that they were there.

Mrs. Alvey was the first one to think that there might be some basis for her son's fears.

One day as she was collecting dirty clothes from Brian's closet for the weekly wash, she noticed something on the floor by the back wall. She looked closer and saw that it was black dirt. It wasn't like the dirt in the yard. Where had it come from?

Puzzled, she cleaned it up. She wondered if something really was getting through the wall somehow and scaring Brian. She couldn't see any holes, but the dirt had to have come from somewhere.

She mentioned the incident to Mr. Alvey, but he had no explanation, either.

The next afternoon, Mrs. Alvey was shopping for groceries when she met two of her neighbors. They stopped to chat, and asked if she was having any problems settling in.

During the conversation, Mrs. Alvey casually mentioned that something seemed to be getting into Brian's closet. She asked if they had ever had problems with animals getting inside their houses.

"No," they told her, "nothing has ever gotten in."

Mrs. Alvey's story had piqued their curiosity and they encouraged her to elaborate. Without thinking about it, she told them all about Brian's problem with the Creepy Crawlies. They were sympathetic, but neither could offer much help.

One did remember that an old coal mine used to provide jobs for men in the area a long time ago.

"The mine was closed years ago," she said. "Several men were trapped and died when there was an explosion in one of the tunnels. Instead of trying to reopen, the company sold the land for a housing development. I don't think your house is close to the mine, but it might be possible that rats got in the mine shafts and tunneled through."

Mrs. Alvey shuddered at such a repulsive idea. She quickly assured them that there were no rats in her house. She thanked the ladies and returned home, wishing she'd never brought up the subject.

That night, she listened by the closet door after she tucked Brian in. She couldn't be sure, but she thought she heard a soft scraping on the floor. She waited a minute, but she heard nothing else. When she caught up with her work, she might call an exterminator to come out and take a look.

Brian hadn't mentioned the sounds in the closet for days, and the dreams weren't coming as often.

Just as Mrs. Alvey began to think the ordeal might be over, trouble came from an unexpected source.

Brian came home from the first day of school crying and saying he was never going back. He was so furious with his mother, he ran to his room and locked the door. He wouldn't come out until his father came home. They finally persuaded him to tell them what had happened.

Word had spread about the Alveys' closet as a result of the grocery store discussion. All the kids at school had heard about Brian's problem. They showed no mercy with their teasing.

"I'm so sorry, Brian! I didn't think the other children would find out," explained Mrs. Alvey. "I was just trying to get some information."

"You shouldn't have told," sobbed Brian.

"They'll probably forget all about it by tomorrow," said Mrs. Alvey. "Just don't let them see that it bothers you."

They didn't forget. They made fun of him all the next day.

"What's in your closet, Brian?" they jeered. "Are they killer teddy bears or stinky old rats?"

Some of them even got down and crawled around on their stomachs.

"Is this the way the Creepy Crawlies do it?" they giggled.

Now Brian began to hate the days as much as the nights. He began to lose sleep and weight. The sneering of the kids at school and the scraping of the Creepy Crawlies at home tormented him constantly.

Mrs. Alvey didn't see any more black dirt, but she now smelled a damp, musty odor in the closet when she gathered Brian's clothes for the wash.

One night when she brought in the clean clothes to hang in the closet, she was overwhelmed by an urge to run. She actually retreated from the door. She felt foolish for being so scared. She grabbed the closet door and yanked it open.

Maybe it was just her eyes, but it looked to her like several shadowy forms vanished through the wall. Something had to be getting inside. She didn't care how expensive exterminators were, she was going to find out what was going on.

She ran straight to the phone and dialed the No Pest Company. She asked for someone right away, but the only time they had available was on Monday. She set up the appointment, but she worried that she had waited too long. Whatever was in the closet was getting stronger.

On Saturday morning, Mr. and Mrs. Alvey tried to persuade Brian to go shopping with them. He didn't like going out much any more, because he was afraid of running into the kids from school. He decided to stay home alone and watch TV.

His parents had just left when Brian heard the doorbell ring. He looked out, but he didn't see anyone. He opened the door and stepped outside. From around the corner dashed his daily tormentors from school, who pushed him inside before he could close the door.

"You can't come in here!" said Brian. "I'll call my dad!"

"We're already in!" they laughed. "We saw your folks leave, so we came to see the Creepy Crawlies!"

They crossed the living room and strolled down the hall, opening doors until they found Brian's room.

"Wait!" called Brian. "Don't go in there."

The boys only laughed. They were already going through the door.

Brian followed, torn by the urge to throw them out and by the need for them to hear the Creepy Crawlies and know that he was telling the truth.

Brian walked to the closet door. He could hear something moving inside.

"Listen!" he said. "They're in there now!"

The boys gathered around Brian, and before he realized what was happening, they grabbed him and pushed him into the closet. He heard the key turn in the lock, and he heard them rolling around on the floor, laughing and howling.

Then something very, very cold began pulling at Brian from the closet wall.

Brian screamed and kicked and pounded, but he couldn't open the door. None of the kids would let him out. The more he begged, the harder they laughed.

Then the room got cold and the sounds in the closet ceased. The kids stopped laughing.

"Maybe he fainted," someone said. "We'd better let him out."

They unlocked the door, expecting to see a very frightened boy. Instead, they saw only clothes and toys and some specks of black dirt on the wall. Brian was gone.

They stood staring at the spot where they had seen him just minutes ago. It had seemed like such a good joke then, but nobody was laughing now.

"He's hiding," said one of the boys. "There must be a hidden door in the wall or the floor."

They looked, but they didn't find one. They called his name, but they got no answer. This was not at all what they had planned. They were still searching for him when his parents came home.

Mr. Alvey knew what they had done before they told him. He was sure they had meant no harm, but he was completely baffled about Brian's disappearance. He thought at first that the boys were right about Brian's hiding. He couldn't imagine where he could be.

After they had completely searched the house without a trace of Brian, Mr. Alvey had to admit that something was seriously wrong. Mrs. Alvey and the boys looked outside while Mr. Alvey phoned the police.

The police responded quickly, but their investigation turned up nothing. They questioned the boys and sent them home.

After they had gone, Mrs. Alvey told the officers the story about the closet. She repeated the conversation she had had with the two women about the old mine.

"Do you think there is any connection between the old mine and Brian's disappearance?" she asked.

"No," said the first officer. "There's nothing down in that mine but a bunch of dead men."

The shafts and the tunnels wouldn't reach this far," said the second policeman, "unless those dead men have been digging a long time. Try not to worry. We'll find the boy."

The hours dragged by with no news of Brian, and the Alveys lost all sense of time while they waited.

Mrs. Alvey realized it was Monday when the exterminator from No Pest came. She hadn't thought to cancel the appointment.

"I don't need you now," she thought bitterly.

"Since you're here, you might as well have a look around," said Mr. Alvey.

The exterminator checked the house inside and out, but there was no evidence of anything. Before leaving, he decided to crawl under the floor to be sure he hadn't missed anything. There were no signs of any animals or any breaks in the ground. All he saw was a lump of coal and a rusty old miner's hat with a burned out light on top. He kicked them out of the way. They were not worth mentioning, and they were the only things he found beneath the closet.

Night Voice

"Help me, please! I'm hungry!"

The voice came faintly to camp through the darkness. It was the second time Adam Quimby had heard it, but tonight he wasn't going to do what he'd done last night.

Last night when the voice called, he had run from his cabin and told the counselors.

They had listened, but had assured him they'd heard nothing at all.

He could still hear the voice. Surely they could, too. When he'd insisted that someone was calling for help, they'd laughed at him and told him to go back to bed and stop being such a baby.

At breakfast, they told the whole camp about Adam's night voice, and everybody teased him for the rest of the day.

After that humiliation, Adam was never going to give them an opportunity to make fun of him again.

He tried to sleep, but the eerie sound continued.

"Help me, please! I'm hungry!"

Adam pulled the covers tighter to shut out the voice, but he was unsuccessful.

"I'm hungry! Please help me!" it called again, somewhere close to camp.

Scott Ashley sat up in the next bunk.

"What was that?" he whispered.

"Probably some jerk trying to tease me again about last night," said Adam.

Scott turned on his flashlight. Adam could see that his eyes looked big and round and frightened.

"Is that what you heard last night?" Scott asked.

"Exactly," said Adam.

"Do you know who that sounds like?" Scott whispered in an awe-stricken voice.

"No," replied Adam. "Who?"

"It sounds like Ralph King," Scott answered. "He had your bunk last year. All he thought about was eating. He stole most of the food my mom sent me from home."

"Sounds like a nerd," said Adam.

"Yeah," said Scott. "Nobody liked him, but nobody wanted anything really bad to happen to him."

"Wasn't that the boy who got lost in the cave?" inquired Adam, sitting up.

"Yeah," said Scott, "but he didn't exactly get lost."

A little shiver went unexpectedly up Adam's spine, and he pulled his blanket around his shoulders.

"What happened?" he asked Scott.

"It's hard to say for sure," said Scott. "Two of the counselors took some of us on a night hike through the cave. They gave us a long rope to hold onto. We were supposed to stay together in a single line, but Ralph turned loose of the rope and climbed up on a big rock. The counselors saw him and told him to come down, and it looked like he started to. He turned toward us and then he was just gone. It didn't look like he fell. It looked like the rock just gobbled him up. Something must have snatched him. It happened so fast, we couldn't tell. We got out of there as fast as we could."

"Didn't you look for him?" asked Adam.

"Well, sure," said Scott, "of course we did! And we had help from the police and other people. But we couldn't find a hole behind the rock. We couldn't see anything."

"It must have been awful," said Adam.

"It was," Scott agreed. "We heard this crunching when his body vanished, but we never did hear it hit the bottom. We could hear him screaming at first, but that didn't last long. We called and called, but he never made another sound. I guess he was already dead by then. I'd sure hate to have to stay in that cave forever like poor Ralph."

"You mean they never got his body out?" Adam asked, surprised by this morbid information.

"No," said Scott. "There was no trace of him."

Adam made no comment. Both boys sat thinking about the horror of being lost in a cave like poor Ralph King.

The ghostly voice broke the silence again.

"Help me, please! I'm hungry!"

Adam and Scott looked at each other and shivered. It sounded so pitiful.

"I tell you, it sounds just like him," said Scott.

"I've been thinking," said Adam. "What if he didn't die?"

"What?" asked Scott, startled by the suggestion.

"What if he managed to survive somehow?"said Adam.

"That's impossible!" exclaimed Scott. "Even if he survived the fall, he would've starved to death by now!"

"Maybe he ate raw fish or his own arm or something," suggested Adam.

They laughed, picturing a boy gnawing on his own arm.

"I've read stories about things like that," Adam went on. "From what I hear of Ralph, he'd be searching for something to munch on."

Scott had become serious again.

"No way," he said. "If you had heard that crunching and that scream, you'd know he *couldn't* look for food."

"Then how do you explain the voice?" asked Adam.

"I can't," said Scott. "Maybe it's his ghost."

"Hunger can make people do weird things," said Adam.

"Dead people don't get hungry," declared Scott.

"They don't call for help either!" said Adam. "It sounds to me like he's alive."

"Maybe you're right," Scott conceded. "We're not just hearing things. There is definitely somebody out there calling."

The voice came again, as if on cue.

"Help me, please! I'm hungry!"

"It's coming from the direction of the cave," said Scott. "I think we ought to tell the counselors."

"No!" Adam insisted. "They'd just laugh again. They couldn't do anything that we couldn't do. Maybe we should just forget the whole thing and get some sleep."

Before they could pull up the covers, the voice came again through the darkness, more urgent than ever.

"Please help me! I need something to eat!"

The boys crept to the door and listened.

"Please!" the voice called louder.

Adam turned to Scott.

"Get dressed," he told him. "We've got to find out where that voice is coming from."

Scott hesitated.

"Come on!" urged Adam. "You've got to show me where Ralph disappeared in the cave."

"I don't think that's a good idea," Scott protested.

"What if you were out there calling?" asked Adam. "Wouldn't you want somebody to help you?"

"Well, yes," said Scott. "But I think we should take somebody with us."

"There's no time," said Adam. "Hurry!"

The boys pulled on their clothes, grabbed their flashlights, and headed toward the cave. The voice kept calling at intervals. As they walked down the trail, they could hear it more clearly. There was no doubt now that it was coming from inside the cave.

"Has all of this cave been explored?" asked Adam.

"I doubt it," said Scott. "Nobody even knew about it until a few years ago. Some big rocks had always sealed the entrance. One day they fell off in a storm or something, and there was the entrance to the cave."

"How big is it?" Adam wanted to know.

"I don't know," said Scott. "We didn't get to go very far. The part we were in was like a big room. There was this huge rock sticking out from the side. It was the one Ralph climbed on."

"What did the rock look like?" quizzed Adam.

"I never saw one like it before," Scott answered. "Our lights that night made it look like a scaly monster."

Adam shuddered. He wasn't so sure he wanted to see it after all, but it was too late to turn back.

They continued down the trail without talking. They soon reached the entrance and stopped.

The voice spoke at once, as if it knew that they were there.

"Help me, please! I'm hungry!"

Adam and Scott shined their flashlights inside the cave entrance. The walls were smooth with strange markings, but nothing moved. Cautiously, they stepped inside and looked around.

"Which way did you go that night?" whispered Adam.

"That way," Scott whispered back, pointing straight ahead.

Shining their lights in front of them, they walked only a short distance before Scott stopped.

"There it is," he said.

They were standing in front of a massive rock beside the passageway. It did appear scaly in the dim light, but Adam could detect no openings.

"Are you sure that's where Ralph fell?" asked Adam.

As Scott nodded his head, the voice boomed out from behind the rock.

"I'm hungry!"

The boys nearly dropped their lights as they jumped back and collided. The voice was so near that they half expected Ralph King to come climbing out of a crevice.

Adam regained his composure and stepped closer to the rock. He put one foot against it and pushed. It seemed secure. He would have stepped up on it with the other foot, but Scott yanked him back.

"Are you nuts?" he said. "That's what Ralph did!"

"Oh, right," said Adam. "It looks safe enough, though."

"I guess that's what Ralph thought," Scott reminded him, "but look what happened."

Adam thought for a moment. He examined the rock and then turned to Scott.

"Here, hold my light," he said. "I want to try something."

"What are you going to do?" asked Scott.

"I'm going to climb up and lie on my stomach so I won't lose my balance and fall. I think I can stretch far enough to see if there is an opening behind the rock."

"Be careful," Scott cautioned. "There's something strange here."

Adam climbed up and lay down. Scott directed the light on him as he inched his way along the rock to the spot where Ralph had vanished.

Something scraped, like rocks rubbing together.

"Ralph!" Adam called. "Are you down there?"

His own words echoed back to him, but no other voice spoke—not even Scott's.

Adam looked back at Scott to double check the location, but Scott was staring with horror beyond Adam. Adam whirled and looked in the same direction, but he was too late.

The rock he was lying on was opening. Jagged teeth lined both sides, and a deep purple tongue shot from below, wrapping itself around Adam in a flash before he could move. As it pulled him down, Adam began to scream and the rock snapped shut.

Scott heard the same crunching sound he'd heard the year before coming from the rock. He turned and ran from the cave, waving both flashlights and screaming for the counselors. He tried to shut out the sounds that followed him.

Inside the cave, a voice in the night burped and breathed a deep sigh of satisfaction.

Up For Grabs

Robert Mitchell was not the kind of man to whom unusual things happened. He had lived such an ordinary life that he didn't know how to cope when unusual things did occur.

During his twenty-year marriage, Robert had built his farm into a profitable business. His life had followed a well-planned routine. Robert would eat a hearty breakfast prepared by his wife, and then he'd go about the business of the day. He thought about no other women and none thought about him because he was so devoted to his wife.

Then Robert's life changed without warning. His wife died, and he was up for grabs.

Robert had always thought that he would die first, so he never planned on dating again. Now every single woman around brought him cakes and casseroles and dinner invitations, and they scared poor Robert half to death.

He was relieved when they gave up and stopped coming over.

Robert did like to eat, though, so he began driving down the highway to the little diner for his morning meal.

The diner was owned and run by the widow Mazie Malone. She found Robert attractive, even if he was set in his ways. She made it her personal business to see that Robert was well fed. The other farmers who gathered in the diner to eat the homemade pancakes, biscuits, eggs, sausage, and gravy began to tease Robert because his portions were always bigger than theirs.

"Mazie's after your body!" they joked.

Robert liked getting full measure for his money, and he was flattered by Mazie's attention. She wasn't the most beautiful woman he'd ever seen, but she was attractive in a neat sort of way. He was fascinated because she could talk about anything, and she always knew what he was thinking.

"Mazie," he said, "I think you've got me bewitched."

The two settled into a comfortable relationship.

Robert was content again and totally unprepared for the next thing that happened.

Millie Swanson moved down from the North.

Millie eyed the prosperous farm and the farmer, twenty years her senior, and decided it would be to her advantage to have both.

She said all the things to Robert that a man of forty-eight would want to hear from a woman twenty years younger. Robert was so flattered he couldn't believe his luck.

"Beware!" warned Mazie. "She's a schemer."

"You're just jealous!" said Robert. "Millie's only a friend."

Mazie hoped that Robert would come to his senses, but as his calls came less and less frequently, she knew this was not going to happen. When he did call, most of the conversation consisted of stories about his friend Millie.

Mazie knew that something more than friendship had developed when Robert stopped coming to the diner for breakfast. She could hear the men laughing and talking behind her back, and she was terribly hurt.

She was still hurting when Robert called later to tell her all the things he and Millie had been doing.

"I don't want to know about Millie," she said. "I want to know about us."

Robert was feeling a little guilty about the way he had treated Mazie, so he took the defensive.

"I want us to be friends," he said.

"Well, I don't," she sobbed. "We were more than friends until that girl half your age came along. You are making a fool of yourself and me, too. You can't have us both in your life. One has got to go!"

Robert was angry now, because he recognized some truth in what she said, and he wasn't ready to face it.

"The only way I'd ever want you," Robert said sarcastically, "would be if it was the middle of the night and I was desperate!"

With their anger vented, they were left with nothing to say. Mazie was too hurt to speak.

"I'm sorry," Robert said finally. "I shouldn't have said that. I hate to see it end this way. Can't we at least be friends?"

"No," said Mazie quietly. "I'll just wait. Maybe you will be desperate sometime in the middle of the night. Then I'll come to you."

The receiver clicked down, and Robert sat there with the strangest feeling he'd ever had in his life. There was something in Mazie's voice that he'd never heard before. He had the saddest feeling that he'd never see her again.

He thought several times about calling, but Millie was always there with something planned for them to do. While Robert was under the impression that Millie wasn't serious, he began to hear the little hints that warned him another change might be on its way.

He wanted to ask the men who ate at the diner how Mazie was doing, but they all avoided the subject. Robert's rejection had shattered and humiliated Mazie. They saw how depressed she was, but they didn't know how to help her.

One morning when they arrived at Mazie's diner, it wasn't open. The door was locked and there was no sign of her. They hoped she had just gone somewhere, but they expected the worst when they called for the police and a doctor. They found her in her bed. Her heart had just stopped beating.

Robert was stunned when he heard the news. He was more deeply affected by Mazie's death than he had ever imagined possible.

Millie was not in the least sympathetic. She increased the hints about marriage until Robert told her straight out that he wasn't ready for that. Millie decided he might never be ready, so she packed up and moved back home.

Robert was alone again, and this time there was no Mazie to give him support. Even though Millie had once made him feel young, she'd left him feeling old and unwanted.

The diner opened again under new management, and Robert eventually began going back every morning. It wasn't the same, but he needed to be around people.

At first, the men only talked about the crops and the weather. Then they began to talk about Mazie. Robert felt so guilty about hurting her that, one morning, he told the men about the cruel things they had said to each other the last time they had talked.

The men treated it lightly.

"She was always after your body," they said. "Maybe she'll come back and get you some night."

There were times when Robert almost believed it might happen. Not long after he talked to the men, things happened that he couldn't explain.

Several times he'd driven by the diner after the new owner had closed, and he'd seen a light on in Mazie's old room.

Once the phone rang about the time of night that Mazie had died, and it had sounded like a woman sobbing when he answered. Then the line had gone dead.

Unnerving things began happening when Robert was out of his house. He'd come home and find his bed rumpled as if someone had been on it while he was gone. Sometimes his clothes would be moved from where he'd left them.

He didn't dare tell anyone about the odd things that were going on. The men at the diner would either laugh at him or think he was crazy.

One morning, Robert woke up to the smell of coffee and bacon frying in the kitchen. He rushed downstairs, but nothing was there. Lights came on and off by themselves, and a couple of nights, he thought he heard the front door open and close after he had locked it.

He had nobody to talk to, and he began to feel very desperate.

On such a night, he woke at midnight—exactly in the middle of the night—and heard soft footsteps coming up the stairs. He knew nobody else was in the house, yet he could hear the footsteps distinctly, and they were heading for his room.

He tried to think what to do. He should be dressed if he had to confront an intruder. He sat up and pulled on his old jeans. Then he crept to the door and waited.

The steps were light, and just before the door opened, he caught the scent of the perfume Mazie used to wear. Before he could move, two hands reached up and grabbed him. The hands he'd held many times pulled him down the stairs and out the door.

Robert didn't show up at the diner that day, but the men thought nothing of it. He was probably busy with the harvest. The second day, when he didn't show up, they became concerned. They drove out to the farm to be sure he was all right.

When they arrived the door was standing open, but there was no sign of Robert in the house. They checked the barn, but he wasn't there.

Then one of the men noticed a strip of mashed grass that reached from the porch to the edge of the yard by the cornfield. Something had been dragged through the yard. The men followed a trail of broken cornstalks through the field until they came to the old road that led to the cemetery.

From the road, they could see that Mazie's grave had been disturbed. Something had been flung across the headstone. It was not until they were very close that they recognized Robert's old jeans. They tried not to think about why they were there.

Then one of them noticed that something was half buried by the dirt in the grave. They all approached for a closer look. They saw two hands—hands they all knew, for they had seen them many times holding a cup of coffee down at Mazie's diner. There was no doubt that the hands were Robert's. This time, instead of coffee, they were holding fistfuls of dirt, as if they had grabbed the earth in a desperate attempt to hang on.

Frantically, the men began to take the dirt away to uncover the body. When they finished, they saw the unbelievable—something they would never have expected in a million years. Robert Mitchell's hands were not attached to anything.

Pop-Ups

"Whooo!"

"What was that?" asked Cory Crawford.

"Just an owl," said Jeff Elgin.

The boys had been to a party at a friend's house, and they were walking through the woods on a short-cut home.

"Whooo!"

"Maybe it's those dead men calling Hoot Cartou!" said Cory.

"You didn't believe that stupid story, did you?" sneered Jeff.

"Naw, I was just kidding," said Corey.

Actually, the story he heard at the party scared him a little. It was supposed to have happened in these very woods a long time ago. He wouldn't let Jeff know, but he remembered every word.

The story began as Abe Riley, Amos Ambrose, and Hoot Cartou were returning from a successful trip to town, where they had sold all the furs they had trapped, and wound up with their pockets brimming with money.

They camped for the night, and Abe and Amos went to sleep right away.

Hoot Cartou stretched out on a log across from Abe and Amos, and he let his thoughts drift back to the sounds and the smells of town. He was getting tired of living in the woods and sleeping on hard logs. He wanted to lie on soft mattresses the way he had last night. He wanted to hear people laughing and singing instead of Abe and Amos snoring. He'd need much more money than his share from this trip before he could live in town.

"I could just take it all," he thought. "I could head out while they're asleep."

The more he thought about it, the more he liked the idea.

Abe and Amos didn't stir as he pulled the money from their pockets and stuffed it in his own. He untied his horse and started to mount, but the horse snorted and pulled back, snapping a dead branch by the trail.

Abe and Amos roused up at the noise and saw in one glance what was going on. They reached for their guns, but Hoot fired two shots first. He didn't mean to kill them, but they would have shot him if he hadn't. He had no time for regret. He had to dispose of the bodies and move on. If anybody asked about them, he'd say they'd gone off on their own. Since they had no family, it wasn't likely that anyone would ask.

Digging graves was harder than he thought. The clearing where they had camped was small, and it hardly provided space for two grave sites. He decided to dig straight down, put Abe and Amos in feet first, and cover the grave with big rocks.

Hoot scanned the clearing for the kind of rocks he needed, but he soon realized there were none big enough to serve his purpose. He started to look for some off the trail, but he heard something moving in the bushes.

"Maybe somebody saw me," he thought.

He had to find out if there was a witness. He ducked behind the nearest tree and listened. It was coming closer and it was coming fast.

It came from among the trees into the moonlight, and Hoot saw it was an animal. He couldn't see clearly from behind the tree, but he knew it was big and it was coming right toward him. For the second time that night, he pointed his gun and fired two shots.

The animal fell and lay still. Hoot came from his hiding place behind the tree and approached cautiously. He swore at himself with disgust.

"A cow," he said. "I've shot a skinny old cow that wandered away from some farm looking for food! Now I'll have some farmer after me!"

And now he'd have to get rid of the cow, too!

He was trying to muster the strength to dig another grave, when the answer to his problem came to him. He'd put her on top of Abe and Amos. Then if anybody found the grave, they'd think it only held the cow's remains.

Hoot pulled and tugged and finally managed to drag the dead cow to the edge of the grave. He glanced down, jumped back and fell over the cow.

He had been startled to see the two heads popped up through the loose layer of dirt that he had shoveled over them. The dirt must have settled or slid off. The two pairs of eyes were open and staring right at him.

He couldn't stand it! He scrambled to his feet and scooped chunks of earth over them again. He pushed the cow into the grave and finished filling it in. Then he searched the woods until he found three rocks big enough to cover the grave.

Taking the money and the horses, Hoot left for the city.

The morning after the killings, the farmer and his two sons came through the woods, looking for the stray cow. They followed her trail to the clearing, where the tracks stopped.

"Look," the farmer told his boys. "This looks like a grave!"

They moved the rocks and raked the dirt away, and there was their missing cow. They pulled her out to examine her, and up popped the heads of Abe and Amos! Frightened out of their wits, they nearly trampled each other running for the sheriff.

"Hoot! Hoot! Hoot Cartou!" the heads called after them.

The sheriff and his men found it hard to believe their story about the heads, but they returned with the farmer and his sons to the clearing.

They saw the cow on the ground, but nothing else.

"Hoot! Hoot! Hoot Cartou!"

"Hear that?" asked the farmer. "The dead men are calling the killer!"

"Take it easy," said the sheriff. "That's just an old owl saying 'Whoo! Whoo! Whoo are you!' I've heard them all my life."

He motioned his men forward, but they were stopped by a rumbling underground, ahead on the path. The earth broke open, and up popped two heads.

"Hoot!" they called in unison. "Hoot Cartou!"

"See, I told you," said the farmer, "I told you it wasn't an owl!"

Nobody was listening. Every man in the group turned and ran from the woods. The farmer was close behind, fully expecting the heads to roll along beside them.

Nobody ever saw Hoot Cartou again, but the heads stay in the woods, waiting and watching. Hardly anybody ever walks through those woods at night, because they don't want to see Abe and Amos.

Corey had just thought the story through, when the hooting started again.

"I guess that was a pretty goofy story," said Corey.

"Yeah," said Jeff. "I don't know how anybody can believe anything so silly!"

The hooting sounded again, very close behind them. Jeff and Corey didn't look back, so they didn't see the two heads pop up from the ground and look at them to see if they were Hoot Cartou!

Betty's Light

Daniel Campbell and his friends, Carl Turner and Eddie Foster, sat by their campfire, glancing nervously over their shoulders from time to time at the dark woods beside the field where they had pitched their tent.

Daniel's father had helped them set up camp beside a little stream that ran along his property line. After they got the fire going, Mr. Campbell gave the boys final safety instructions and turned to go. As he did, a light came on in Betty Moppins's old house in the adjoining field.

"Stay on my land," he told the boys. "Don't do anything to bother that old lady."

The three boys agreed to do as they were told, so Mr. Campbell said good night and left the boys alone.

At first, they sat quietly and watched the flames devour the twigs and small branches before leaping to the larger pieces of wood. In the distance, Betty's tiny light flickered in her window. Other than the firelight and Betty's light, there was nothing but total darkness.

An owl hooted in the woods, and the boys inched closer in their circle.

When the boys had first planned the overnight camping, ghost tales had been on their agenda. Now, with the warm, green woods shrouded in darkness, none of the three felt brave enough for a scary story. Instead, they began to talk about Betty Moppins.

"Do you think she really buries her money in fruit jars around her farm?" asked Eddie.

"Oh, yes," said Daniel. "My mother says she doesn't trust anyone since somebody stole her hams from the smokehouse several years ago. I guess she's afraid somebody will steal her money if she doesn't hide it."

"I can't imagine her being afraid of anything," said Carl. "My father says she's not afraid of the devil himself. I wouldn't be either if I had that gun of hers. It's a real beauty."

"I feel kind of sorry for her," said Daniel. "She doesn't have any family or friends—not even visitors. I wouldn't want to live that way."

"Me neither," said Eddie.

"I might for enough money," said Carl. "How much do you think she's got?"

"It surely isn't much," said Eddie. "Look at that old house she lives in."

"You can't go by that," Carl told him. "We all live in good houses, but we don't have much money."

The others nodded in agreement, and the three sat quietly, thinking and watching the fire die down. Each was imagining how nice it would be to be rich.

Carl was the first to speak.

"Let's have a treasure hunt," he suggested to the others.

"Great!" agreed Daniel and Eddie.

The idea was much more appealing than conjuring up ghosts or discussing strange old women.

"Here's what we'll do," said Eddie. "We'll pretend that this field is a deserted island and that we've come here looking for pirates' treasure."

"Yeah," said Daniel.

"No!" Carl interrupted. "I mean a real treasure hunt."

"A real treasure hunt?" Daniel repeated. "You don't mean Betty's money, do you?"

"That's exactly what I mean," Carl continued. "Looking for pirates' treasure is kids' stuff."

"It's too risky," said Daniel.

"Yeah," said Eddie. "What if she catches us? You know we're not supposed to bother her."

"She'll never know we've been there," explained Carl. "We'll wait for her light to go out and then we'll give her time to go to sleep before we go over to dig."

"We don't even have a shovel," said Eddie, still uncertain about the plan of action.

"We can use those sharp rocks by the stream," said Carl.

Daniel and Eddie couldn't think of any more objections, so they both looked at Carl and nodded.

With excitement building, the boys sat and waited.

The moon came up over the trees, but they hardly noticed. The fire had almost burned itself out, but they made no move to add wood. They sat while uneasy, restless feelings crept along their spines.

After what seemed like hours, Betty's light went out. The boys forced themselves to wait several more minutes to be sure that she was sound asleep.

Picking up rocks from the bank, they crossed the stream and looked around for a place to dig.

"The ground looks sunk in a little here," said Daniel. "This might be a good place to start digging."

The boys dropped to their knees and began to scoop away the top layer of dirt with their rocks. The soil was loose, so they worked quickly. They hadn't dug very deep when their rocks scraped against something. They dug faster and uncovered a jar—a jar full of money. They couldn't believe their luck!

They stood up and danced around, passing the jar back and forth in an effort to see how much was in it. The moonlight wasn't bright enough to tell, but the jar was full.

The boys had planned the hunting, not the finding. They were so excited, they forgot to keep their voices low. The sound carried across the field and woke Betty. They didn't hear her coming until she was right on them. Whirling around, they faced the old woman and fell silent. The barrel of a gun pointed straight at them left their mouths dry and speechless.

"Give me my money, you trespassing little thieves!" screeched Betty. "I ought to shoot the lot of you!"

The boys stood rooted to the ground. Daniel was clutching the jar with both hands, so Betty turned the gun toward him.

"Give me my money!" she demanded again.

Thinking she was going to shoot, Eddie panicked. With a lunge, he hit the gun, knocking the barrel upward. The sudden motion caught Betty off balance. She staggered and fell, striking her head against a rock in the shallow stream. She lay there motionless.

The boys rushed to her. They patted her face, splashed her with water, and tried to get her to speak. There was no response.

"Oh, no," Eddie wailed. "I think she's dead! What'll we do?"

They knew they had to do something fast, but they looked at each other in confusion, each hoping the other would come up with an answer.

They'd never meant to hurt her. They knew what serious trouble they were in. It would have been bad enough just to be caught bothering her, but now they'd killed her and something terrible would happen to them.

Finally, Daniel spoke.

"This might work," he said. "Eddie and I will carry her to her house. Carl will put the money back and leave the gun over by our tent before he goes for help. We'll tell our folks that she came over complaining about our noise and fell."

The boys agreed that that would be the best thing to do. Daniel and Eddie picked up the old lady and carried her to her house, leaving Carl to bury the money, move the gun, and get help.

Carl watched them until they were halfway across the field, and then he dumped the money in his knapsack. He covered the empty jar and put rocks over the smooth earth. Then he went for help.

The news of Betty's death spread quickly, and by early the next day, all the neighbors had gathered at Betty's place.

According to local custom, the body was prepared for burial at home. The women dressed the corpse while the men made the coffin in Daniel's father's barn. Since

Betty had no relatives to contact, those gathered decided to go on with the funeral at once.

A few words were said and the people filed by to view Betty for the last time. The boys stared in guilt and fascination at the still form lying in the coffin. Suddenly, Eddie grabbed Carl's arm.

"Did you see that?" he said in a frantic whisper. "She moved! I swear it! She pointed her finger right at us."

"Don't be stupid," Carl hissed back. "Dead people don't point. Just shut up!"

Daniel's father overheard the boys.

"Sometimes dead people do move as they stiffen," he told them. "You witnessed a terrible thing. Try to put it out of your minds."

They tried, but they couldn't stop thinking about all that had happened. They trembled as they watched the men nail the lid on the old woman's coffin and lower it into the ground. All of this tragedy was their fault. Betty Moppins would still be alive if they hadn't gone on that treasure hunt. Their guilt was crushing.

What if Eddie had been right about seeing her move in the coffin? Daniel wondered. Was it possible to bury someone alive?

He didn't think so. He turned and followed the others out of the graveyard.

About two weeks after Betty's funeral, school began. Daniel had seen Eddie several times during those two weeks, but Carl had kept his distance from both of them. At school, the three of them had classes together, but Carl always had an excuse if they asked him to do something with them when class was over.

They noticed that Carl had more money to spend than usual. One day Eddie came running to tell Daniel that he'd seen Carl with a new gun. He'd never been able to afford one before.

Daniel didn't want to believe what he was thinking.

"He kept the money!" said Eddie, voicing Daniel's thoughts. "I'm scared! I know something will happen!"

The next day, something did. Stories began to circulate that Betty's ghost had been seen carrying her light, going from the graveyard to the farm to check on all the places where she'd buried her money. The stories kept most people out of the area at night, but some still came out of curiosity and insisted that they saw her light moving along the road.

Daniel and Eddie began spending as much time together as possible. Each sighting placed the light nearer to the boys.

One night they were upstairs at Daniel's house watching their old campsite from the window. That's when they saw it. A light came along the stream and stopped at the very spot where they had found the jar filled with money. Then it turned and floated toward Daniel's house. Eddie and Daniel closed the curtains and jumped under the bed covers. Neither was brave enough to look out again.

The next day at school, they were surprised when Carl came up to them before class.

"I thought you guys might want to come over to my place tonight," he said.

He was pale and looked as if he hadn't slept.

"You saw her last night, too, didn't you?" asked Daniel.

"Saw who?" Carl answered, but his face turned a shade paler, and Daniel knew he was right.

"You took the money," said Eddie. "That's why you've been avoiding us. You've got to give it back! That's what she's looking for. She won't stay in her grave until she gets it."

Carl didn't deny it. He was trembling now.

"You've got to help me," he said. "I don't know what to do. The light came right up to my window. I was never so scared in my life."

"I think Eddie's right," said Daniel. "You've got to put the money back where we found it."

"I can't," said Carl. "I've spent most of it."

"Then put back what you've got left," said Eddie.

"Will you go with me?" Carl asked. "We could go after school today."

Eddie looked at Daniel and Daniel nodded. The three boys went to class together, just like old times.

After school, they stopped at Carl's house to get the money and a shovel to dig up the empty jar. The fastest way to the spot where it was buried was to cut across Betty's field. They hurried so they could finish before dark.

None of them knew about the old, abandoned well in the field that had been boarded over. They stepped on the boards unawares. Their weight cracked the rotting timber, and the boys plunged to the bottom.

Except for the shock of the fall, they found that they were not hurt. The well was almost dry, so the water came just to their knees. They were in serious trouble nonetheless: the well was too deep for them to climb out. They would need help.

At first they shouted, but then they realized nobody would be within hearing distance.

"When we don't come home tonight, they'll come looking for us," said Daniel. "Then we can make them hear us."

Time passed slowly. None of the boys felt like talking. Finally, it was dark and the boys figured someone would be searching for them. They took turns calling for help, and as the night dragged on, they became frightened and discouraged. When they were about to give up, they heard someone coming. Tears of relief ran down their cheeks.

They looked up and saw a light at the opening. Someone was bending over the edge, looking down at them. They could see by the light that it was the face of a woman—a face they knew only too well.

"No!" they screamed, over and over.

Chunks of rotting flesh fell from her face and splashed into the water. Dirt began to fall from the side of the well and cover the boys. In the light they could see that the hands that dug the dirt were made of nothing but bones.

Lighthouses

I heard the voices down by the beach today. They are getting louder and closer. I hope I'm wrong, but I think I know who they are. The old lighthouse keeper told me they'd be coming; I just didn't think it would be so soon.

He told me that they would try to contact me. I wanted to be prepared for them, but I'm not. I think they know that the old lighthouse won't be saved, and they're moving in already. If they do, the beaches won't be safe for anyone.

I'd be on my way out of here right now, but I'm waiting for my friend Lewis. He thinks we should give it one more try. He hasn't seen them up close the way I have. I know that we can't fight them. There are too many of them and they're too strong. Our only hope is the lighthouse.

Lewis is going to speak to the Historical Beach Society tonight and try to persuade them to find a way to keep the old lighthouse going, but I don't think they'll take him seriously. I think some people think Lewis and I are crazy!

I've heard them talking about us. Some think we are sticking our noses in where we have no business. They say we are outsiders. Others agree with us that the lighthouse should be saved, but they have no idea of how to raise the money to fund the project. If they knew everything that Lewis and I know, they'd find a way. Of course, we can't tell them everything. It would start a panic, or get us locked away.

Lewis and I didn't go searching for information. We only came to the beach for a pleasant vacation. One afternoon, we happened to end up near the old lighthouse with a picnic supper. The old, towering structure looked so magnificent in the twilight that Lewis and I strolled over for a closer look.

The light was fading fast and the lighthouse loomed like a ghost, alone by the sea.

We stood gazing up at first, commenting on how powerful and strong it seemed in spite of its age.

"There's something eternal about it," I said to Lewis.

"Too bad everybody doesn't think so," he said. "I hear they're going to tear it down."

That news made me sad. From the outside, its condition didn't seem to warrant its destruction.

Then Lewis said he'd like to see what it was like inside.

We knew there was a keeper, but we'd never met the old man. He didn't seem to be around.

Lewis opened the door and called out, "Hello!"

At that point, the only sound was the boards creaking under our feet as we ventured a little further inside.

"Hello!" Lewis called again. "Is anybody here?"

This time we heard something move near the window. That's when we found the old lighthouse keeper where he had fallen.

Lewis ran and knelt beside him.

"What happened?" he asked.

The old man rolled his head from side to side.

"Take it easy," said Lewis. "You'll be all right. We'll get you some help."

"Dark!" he said. "Guard!"

"Can you tell me where you hurt?" asked Lewis.

"Dark! Guard!" he repeated.

"He's delirious," I said.

"Maybe," said Lewis, "but I think he's trying to tell us something important."

"We'd better get somebody," I said.

"Right!" Lewis agreed. "Stay with him while I call for help."

I found a small pillow on a chair, and put it under his head.

"Can you tell me your name?" I asked him.

"Keepers!" he mumbled. "All are keepers."

He closed his eyes, rested, and then opened them again. Each time, he would try to speak, but he couldn't make me understand.

I began to think he might die, and I was frightened at the thought that we would be alone. I was relieved when Lewis came back.

"An ambulance is on its way," he said.

"How are you feeling?" I asked the old fellow.

His eyes opened and he looked at Lewis and me. He was lucid and spoke in complete sentences.

"They mustn't destroy the lighthouses," he said. "They guard the entranceways. People don't understand!"

"What don't they understand?" Lewis asked.

The old man's eyes got brighter. His voice was strong with feeling when he answered.

"People think lighthouses are no longer useful. They have fancy equipment to signal ships now. But lighthouses do more than signal the ships out there in the night."

"What do you mean?" I asked.

"Lighthouses have another purpose," he said. "All of us who've kept them know that. They hold back the dark."

"The dark?" I repeated.

"Yes," he continued, "they not only hold back the dark, they hold back what's in the dark. They guard the entrances to this world from the sea."

"What comes from the sea?" I asked, but he didn't answer. His eyes had clouded again.

Lewis and I looked at each other. We were glad that the siren in the distance was getting closer and closer.

The old man did not rouse up again until they were lifting him on the stretcher. Then he opened his eyes and looked at Lewis and me.

"They'll be coming soon," he said to me, "and they'll try to contact you."

I nodded, but I didn't understand then.

Then he said to Lewis, "Promise me you'll keep the light going!"

Lewis promised.

When they had gone with the old man, Lewis looked at me.

"Do you want to climb to the top with me?" he asked. "I want to see what's up there."

High places were not for me.

"No, thank you," I said. "I'll wait outside on the beach."

I didn't realize how dark it had gotten. The water flung itself against the sand, retreated, and came again.

I knew Lewis had not had time to reach the top yet, but it seemed as if he had been gone for hours. I had never been afraid of the dark before, but now I wished that I had gone with Lewis. I felt unseen things creeping along beside me on the sand and I shivered. I walked to the water's edge and stuck my toe in the water.

"There's nothing to be afraid of," I said.

To prove it, I waded in with both feet.

That's when the lighthouse went dark without warning. It was at that exact time, I learned later, that the old keeper had died.

I stood in the water, looking at the sea in the moonlight, and that's when they attached themselves to me. I saw them and I began to scream for Lewis to help me.

I whirled and looked at the lighthouse. Lewis was looking out the small window near the top. I thought he'd run down to me, but I saw him start running back up. I fought and struggled, but the things wouldn't let go. I felt myself being pulled down on the wet sand. The grains rubbed against my face, and then the light was on again, shining in my eyes. The things released me, and I lay exhausted and trembling, panting for breath.

I rolled away from the water and saw the red blotches on my feet and legs. Lewis came running to me from the lighthouse, and I realized then that he had saved me with the light.

Tonight I will wait until Lewis speaks at the meeting. Then we will head inland as far as we can go.

If they vote to destroy the lighthouse, one entrance will be left unguarded. The voices that I heard at the beach will be louder. Out of the sea will come those restless dead, those old, clean-washed bones that will cling to the living like they clung to me that night; the more recently dead, all ghastly and bloated, will march from their watery grave without the guard to hold them back.

If the beach is dark tonight, I want to be far away from the lighthouse.

The Wake-Up Call

Nancy Logan had never had a premonition of danger before the day she accepted the job to replace the missing desk clerk at the Grand Rockport Hotel. As she straightened her skirt and waited at the front desk to greet the first guest, she still felt like she shouldn't be here. But her bank balance told her otherwise, so she checked in the first guest, handed him the key, and rang for the bellhop.

The guest took the key and followed the bellhop to the elevator. Nancy relaxed as she watched. This job might not be so tough, after all.

Nancy looked at her list of things to do. She should probably make sure that the wake-up calls were made first. The night clerk had checked off all except 321. It was due now. She picked up the phone.

A tapping on the desk interrupted her. A little gray-haired lady was staring at her impatiently. Nancy hadn't seen her come in, and she had no idea of how long she had been standing there. It couldn't have been long. It had only taken her a minute to check her list. She decided she'd better make the wake-up call before she got involved with the lady.

"I'll be with you in a minute, ma'am," said Nancy. She gave the lady a bright smile while she punched the numbers.

"I don't have all day!" the lady snapped.

Nancy could hear the phone ringing as she watched the old woman drumming her fingers on the desk.

"That's been ringing long enough to wake the dead," said the woman. "Nobody's going to answer."

Nancy was about to agree and hang up, when someone picked up the receiver. A man's voice spoke, but Nancy couldn't understand what he was saying. He coughed and wheezed between words. Other voices were speaking indistinctly in the background.

"Good morning, sir," said Nancy. "I have a seven o'clock wake-up call for 321. Is everything all right, sir?"

"Ep," the man mumbled. "Room 213."

Nancy was confused. His reply sounded more like "help" than "yep." But if he were ill, surely the other people in the room must be helping him. Had he said Room 213? She was almost positive that he had. If so, she had dialed the wrong number, but she didn't think she had. She'd been very careful.

She started to ask again if she had the right room and if he was all right, but a loud, crackling sound began on the line and she was cut off.

Nancy stood debating whether or not to hang up and try again, but the little old woman at the desk decided for her.

"Are you going to help me, young lady," she asked, "or do I call the manager?"

Nancy hung up the phone.

"I'm sorry, ma'am," she told the lady.

She checked the old woman in, rang for assistance with the luggage, and let out a breath of relief as she watched the disgruntled guest cross the lobby.

Her relief was short-lived.

The phone rang and Nancy picked it up. A man's angry voice surged through the line.

"This is Mr. Carson in 321. What kind of incompetent hotel are you running? I asked for a wake-up call at seven sharp. It's now 7:17! It's lucky I woke up. I'm going to be late as it is!"

He slammed the phone down before Nancy could explain her mistake. He would have still been angry, even with an explanation. Nancy didn't blame him. How could she have mixed up those numbers? The man she'd reached earlier really had said 213! The old woman must have distracted her. Now she'd have to apologize to the man in 213 and to Mr. Carson in 321.

She checked to see who was registered in 213, but she could find no one listed.

Perhaps she'd better explain the whole thing to her supervisor before she made any apologies. She buzzed his office, hoping he'd understand.

"Mr. Hart," she began when he answered, "I've made my first mistake of the day already."

He listened while she explained the mix-up. When he spoke, his voice sounded odd instead of angry.

"Nancy, you couldn't have reached 213. That room is part of the suite that was destroyed by fire last year. We renovated it, but we got so many complaints from guests, we closed it permanently and disconnected the phone."

"I'm sure the man said 213," Nancy insisted.

"You must have misunderstood," he told her, "or the man must have been mistaken about what room he was in."

"Maybe," Nancy conceded reluctantly. In her own mind, she still wasn't convinced.

"Trust me," said Mr. Hart. "Nobody has spent an entire night there since the fire. The guests say they can't sleep, and they insist on being moved to another room."

"Why?" asked Nancy.

"I guess you don't know," he said. "I keep forgetting that you are new in town. A family of four died in that fire."

"No, I hadn't heard about it," said Nancy.

"It was a terrible thing," Mr. Hart continued. "They were asleep. The desk clerk had forgotten to make the wake-up call. He just dropped out of sight after that. I guess he felt that he was responsible."

"Was he the one I replaced?" asked Nancy.

"Yes," replied Mr. Hart. "After he left, a lot of wild stories started going around about 213."

"What kind of stories?" asked Nancy.

"Oh, you know," said Mr. Hart. "The horror tales you'd expect. People that stayed in that room after the fire claimed they heard coughing and wheezing and voices asking for help."

"But that's what I heard when I called!" said Nancy. "Were there any other stories?"

"One guest claimed he saw the desk clerk that used to work here. You know, that kind of nonsense."

"Do you think someone could have sneaked in and could actually be staying up there?" she asked.

"We only use it for storage now," he told her. "People seem to let their imaginations run wild when something like this happens. Just apologize to Mr. Carson and forget it. As you said, it was only a mistake."

Nancy hung up and dialed 321. Mr. Carson didn't answer. She'd try to catch him later and apologize face to face. That would probably be more effective.

She stood there a minute, wondering what would happen if she dialed 213. She decided to try it. She touched the numbers and listened to the ringing on the other end. Someone picked up the receiver again, but the crackling started immediately.

Nancy slammed the receiver down. She had been right! Somebody had answered in that room! Her head began to throb and without knowing why, she reached for a pad and pen and began scribbling. She was surprised to see what she had written: *Wake-up call. Seven o'clock. Room 213.* It didn't even look like her handwriting! The throbbing in her head stopped as suddenly as it had started. She shuddered and tossed the pad on top of some papers in a tray on the desk. Nothing like that had ever happened to her before.

Something odd was going on in this hotel! She was sure that somebody was in that room. She was getting more and more curious about who it could be, and remembered she had a break coming. It surely wouldn't hurt to take a look. The key marked 213 was there, so she took it and hurried to the elevator.

Nobody was in the hall near the door. She was glad of that, for she didn't want anybody to see her. She stood outside 213 and listened for a moment, but she heard nothing. She got a whiff of stale smoke as she bent over to unlock the door. She hesitated. Maybe she ought to forget this. Mr. Hart might not like it if he found out that she had been poking around up here. And she had to admit, she was a little frightened after hearing his stories.

She couldn't stand by the door all day. She had to do something. She compromised. She would open the door and just peek in from the hall.

Turning the knob and pulling the door open was her second mistake of the day.

A blast of hot air sucked her to the center of the room. Flames were all around her, devouring the curtains and carpet. Smoke ate away at her eyes and throat, and she began to cough.

The hotel was on fire! She had to get help! She tried to reach the door, but a wall of heat pushed her back.

A chorus of groans came from behind her, and she turned to see who it was. From the beds rose four black figures, rubbing chunks of charred flesh from their cheeks as they sleepily opened their empty eyes.

A ghostly figure in a desk clerk's uniform crouched in terror near the phone, gasping over and over, "Wake-up call! Wake-up call!"

The smoke and the smell of burning flesh overcame Nancy, and she fell to the floor. The fire crept up slowly at first. Then it leapt on her hungrily, until she was covered by flames.

Mr. Hart wondered why Nancy didn't return from her break. He had waited a while before hiring someone after the fire because he wanted someone dependable. He had thought Nancy was just that. She seemed like such a sensible girl. He must have scared her off with his stories.

Business had picked up, so he had to hire a replacement for Nancy. He hoped this one would be more reliable! He explained the desk clerk's duties to her, and then went into his office.

The new girl reached in the tray for a pad to list the things he'd told her to do. She read the note that Nancy had scribbled. Her head began to throb. She wanted to make a good impression. She wrote down the wake-up call as the very first item on her day's agenda.

Green Thumbs

All Gary Green wanted was to be left alone so he could finish his experiment and leave this town. Obviously, people here watched too many movies about mad scientists. Every kid in the neighborhood had snuck by to try to see what he was doing, and all the adults who fancied they had a green thumb had given him advice about his flower garden. Something had to be done. His project was top secret. He had to have his privacy.

His superiors had anticipated problems with nosy neighbors when they had made the decision to conduct the experiment in a small town. They hadn't realized there would be so many children to deal with.

Gary had chased the Collins kids and the Kimball kids out of his yard for what seemed like the millionth time that day. Their mothers never checked to see what they were doing. Didn't they know that you couldn't be too careful? Bad things happened even in good neighborhoods. He ought to know! He'd had a few close calls himself.

He thought sometimes that the mothers wanted their children to play in his yard, so they'd trample his flowers instead of their own. Maybe they were a little jealous. None of them had green thumbs like his. His yard really was the most beautiful one on the block. The grass on his lawn was greener and thicker, and the flower beds held exotic flowers of brilliant colors.

He'd been using the formula with the new ingredient he'd added at the place he'd lived before coming here. He was running out of the first batch, but he wondered if he dared make another one so soon. Obtaining the special ingredient was always risky. He'd had one of those close calls the last time he did it. He seemed to be on to something, though, and his deadline was approaching.

He needed to work as quickly as possible, but how could he concentrate with all those loud, pesky children running under his windows?

At first, he had asked them politely to stay off his property. They had ignored his request. His next step was to speak to the parents. This had immediately decreased his popularity on the street. Although support had been promised, little had been given. When the kids realized that no punishment would be forthcoming at home, they began to run through his yard on a regular basis. Each time, Gary Green would have to chase them out himself.

The last time he chased the Kimball children, Mrs. Kimball had heard him and had come pounding on his door.

"Mr. Green!" she yelled at him. "I'll thank you not to get after my kids anymore! If they are doing something they shouldn't, you come and let me know, and I'll take care of it!"

"My dear lady," said Gary, "I have already informed you of their misconduct. I can't keep you constantly posted about your children's whereabouts and activities. I merely want them out of my yard, because solitude is necessary for my work."

"Work?" she said. "What work? All I have ever seen you do is piddle around with those flowers. Maybe you ought to spend some time with little children. Then you might see them in a different light."

Gary Green looked at her thoughtfully, and came to a decision. Then he smiled his most charming smile.

"Mrs. Kimball, you may be right. You have given me an idea. Perhaps I will invite the children in to help me with my experiments. I've never used anyone so young before, but they could become part of my project."

Gary Green's sudden change in attitude left Mrs. Kimball at a momentary loss for words.

"Well, good," was all she could finally think of to say.

"Thank you for coming over, Mrs. Kimball," said Gary.

Mrs. Kimball nodded curtly, backed up a couple of steps, turned, and hurried across to her own house.

Gary closed the door quickly and went back to set up the lab for the children. He didn't like this new development, but he couldn't afford to call attention to himself by quarreling with the neighbors. He would have to move faster than he had planned. He was the only one who had progressed this far with the research, and he had to succeed. Too many were depending on him for positive results. His own life would eventually depend on his findings.

Gary Green was working on a fertilizer that could speed up food production for millions of people who were starving. There were similar experiments in progress all across the country, but his combinations were the best, so far. He'd been very daring to try this one special ingredient, but adding it had been the single thing that had made the flowers from back home grow.

Now he was ready to try it again. If it worked this time, he would report it to his superiors and they would begin production on a mass scale.

The potential was good here. Supplies were plentiful. When this hit the market, hunger would be wiped out.

He was ready for the children when he heard their voices in the yard again. The Collins kids and the Kimball kids were back.

He opened the door and called, "Children!"

They heard him and started to scatter to their own yards.

"No, wait!" he called. "Don't go."

They stopped and looked at him, puzzled at the change. Something was fishy here.

"Would you like to come inside and help me with my project?" he asked.

"Are you talking to us?" one of the Collins kids asked.

"Yes," he said. "Really, I could use you. It was Mrs. Kimball's idea. You can check with her if you like."

They were still undecided.

"Of course, I'll understand if you are afraid," he said.

"We're not afraid," they assured him.

He held the door open and they all filed in. Once inside, they were curious about what they would be doing.

"Can we see your lab?" they asked.

"Just follow me," he told them.

He led the children to his lab in the center of the house. He pushed a button and the door slid open. The children saw a room filled with equipment they had never seen before.

"That special compartment in the middle of the lab is what I use for my experiments," he explained. "I am making fertilizer that will grow plants for food."

For once, they were all quiet at the same time. It was like the set of a science fiction movie.

Their curiosity had led them to the special compartment. They looked at him for permission to look inside.

"You may all go inside at once," he said. "It's big enough for all of you. Look around while I enter some data in my computer."

The children stepped inside, amazed at the panel of buttons and blinking lights. Then the door slid quietly closed behind them, and locked.

"This was easier than I expected," thought Gary.

Gary ignored the frightened faces and the frantic beating on the sealed windows. He was glad the compartment was soundproof. These children would make much more noise than the adults he had used before.

Gary Green removed the flesh-colored glove from his right hand, and pushed one button. Rays shot through the compartment, leaving him with an ample supply of the ingredient he needed for his tests.

He took one last look around the place where he had been so successful. Then his green finger and four green thumbs entered the code that would signal the mother ship to come and take him home.

The Egg Hunt

"Did you ever see anything like it?" Jill Maloney asked her older brother Chad. "Do you think this really is an egg?"

Chad shook his head and circled wide around the huge, oval object resting on the ground.

"It's nesting in the bushes," observed Jill, "just like a real egg."

"I don't know what it is," said Chad, "but I don't like it. It gives me the creeps. We've got to tell somebody about this."

"We can't tell!" Jill protested. "Mama will know we've been playing in the woods."

"We could tell her we got lost looking for the Easter eggs Grandpa hid," said Chad.

"No, that wouldn't work," said Jill. "She knows Grandpa didn't hide eggs way back here."

"Yeah, but we could tell her that we didn't know that," he argued.

"Please don't tell," begged Jill. "I think it's an Easter egg, and I want to come back and see it hatch!"

"Whatever it is, it's not an Easter egg, silly!" he said. "It looks kind of spooky to me."

They stood staring at the egg-thing nestled in the bushes near the old, deserted mill pond.

"I wonder how it got here," he said.

"Me, too," said Jill. "I'd hate to see a bird that could lay an egg that big!"

That thought hadn't crossed Chad's mind, and the idea was not one he wanted to dwell on. There couldn't be a bird that big! Of course, he didn't think there could be an egg that big, either, yet there it was.

"Do you think somebody put it here as a trick?" asked Jill.

"No, it's too big for that," he said.

"Then where did it come from?" she asked.

He thought of the huge bird again.

"I don't know, but come on," he said, grabbing her hand. "We're getting out of here."

The children ran back to the edge of the field where they had left the baskets of Easter eggs they'd found on their egg hunt. By the time they reached home, supper was on the table.

Chad and Jill ate and had little to say. Several times, Chad started to tell about the egg in the woods, but Jill's pleading looks stopped him.

Chad wished his father were alive so he could talk to him the way he used to. His mother got too emotional over things. His grandfather had just come to live with them after his father died, so he hadn't been around him long enough to know if he'd understand or not.

The next morning, he was still debating whether or not to tell when he and Jill went outside to play after breakfast. He wanted one more look at the egg-thing before he made up his mind. He didn't want Jill along this time. He sensed something very dangerous about the egg.

He couldn't think of a way to get away from Jill, so he was glad when their dog Murk began barking at a rabbit. When Murk chased after the rabbit, Chad chased after Murk.

The maneuver didn't fool Jill.

"Where are you going?" she called.

"To get the dog," he said.

"I want to go with you," she told him, following along behind him.

"I'll be back in a minute," he said. "Go back and wait."

"You're going to look at the egg, aren't you?" she asked.

"Okay, I'm going to look at the egg! Are you satisfied?" he snarled.

"I'm going, too," she stated.

"I don't want you to go," he said more calmly. "You'll just slow me down."

"I'll tell Mama if you won't let me go!" she threatened.

He had wasted too much time arguing, so he gave in.

"All right, you can go, but you have to keep quiet and do what I tell you," he warned.

Jill agreed, and the two children retraced their steps back into the woods. As they approached the odd nest by the old mill pond, they could see the monstrous egg sticking up above the bushes.

"It's grown!" gasped Jill.

Chad saw she was right, but he said nothing. He needed to get closer to get a better look, but he wasn't sure it was safe. What if it had fallen from space? It might be radioactive or something. He wished there was some way to tell if it was dangerous.

As soon as he formed the wish mentally, it came true. The rabbit Murk was chasing burst through the bushes and headed toward the egg. Murk followed, barking furiously. Both tried to stop near the egg-thing, but the rabbit made a funny gurgling sound, and Murk's barks turned to whines and then yelps of pain. They were pulled toward the egg-thing by some invisible force.

"Murk!" screamed Jill.

She started to run to the dog, and Chad barely had time to stop her. His arm shot out and blocked her, and then he half dragged her down the path toward home.

"It's got Murk," she sobbed. "What is that thing, Chad? Why did it want Murk and the rabbit?"

"I don't know," he said gruffly. "Hurry up! Do you want it to get you, too?"

Jill was still crying when they got home, and this time she didn't object when Chad told their grandfather what had happened.

"I've never heard of such a thing," he said. "Maybe you had better show me where it is so I can take a look."

"Come on," said Chad. "It's down by the pond."

Grandpa Maloney followed the two children along the path.

"It's right beyond those bushes," said Jill. "It's got Murk! Do you think he got away?"

"I don't know, honey," the old man told her. "Let's just have a look."

They were in sight of the nest now. Only one thing had changed since they had been there last: the nest looked empty.

"It's gone!" exclaimed Jill.

"It was there just a few minutes ago, Grandpa. Honest, it was. Where could it be?" said Chad.

"Are you sure you really saw something there?" asked Grandpa. "You didn't just imagine it after watching some scary TV shows, did you?"

"We didn't imagine it, Grandpa," said Jill. "See? The nest is still there. I'll bet it hatched while we were gone!"

Grandpa Maloney took a few steps forward, and he could see large pieces of shell in the nest.

"Wait here," he told the children. "I'm going to look inside it."

They obeyed and watched the old man lean over and look. They saw him begin to retch and then fall forward.

"What's wrong, Grandpa?" Chad shouted, running to the old man, who was gasping for breath.

"Get back! Evil!" he rasped. "Get help! Quick!"

He stiffened, jerked once, and stopped breathing.

Chad ran to the nest and looked in it. A terrible stench that was confined to the broken shells filled his nostrils.

He coughed and gagged.

"Run, Jill!" he said. "Tell Mama to call the sheriff."

She took a step forward.

"Go now!" he screamed at her.

Chad tried to stay conscious until he was sure she wasn't coming to the nest. He didn't want his sister to see the half-absorbed bodies clinging to the pieces of shell. He held on as long as he could and then he fell forward. His last thought was about the egg: what if there were others?

Jill didn't know what to do. She couldn't imagine what had happened to make Jeff and Grandpa fall down the way they did. She didn't want to leave them like that, but it might happen to her, too, if she got too close. Then there would be nobody to go for help. She chose to do what they had told her.

"What could have been in that egg?" she asked herself over and over as she turned to go.

A shadow came across the sky like an answer. Then another came, and another. As they swooped down, she saw huge yellow beaks and sharp, twisted claws. They were the most wicked things she had ever imagined.

Jill ducked into the bushes along the path, hoping they wouldn't spot her. She watched them bank and circle. They knew she was there.

There was no time to tell anyone that there were more eggs out there and that there should be a gigantic egg hunt. She had waited too long.

The eggs had hatched and the hideous things were loose in the world, and they were the hunters now instead of the hunted.

The Craft Shop

Agnes Deverell specialized in the unusual. The little craft shop she managed at the corner of 13th and Main was filled with shelves bulging with homemade brooms, dried flower arrangements, hand-pieced quilts, jewelry carved from bones, and even beautiful baskets covered with dehydrated fruit. For a one-of-a-kind gift, her shop was the place to go.

"You'd think she'd have a fancy name for it," said Charlotte Colter, "instead of just calling it The Craft Shop. That's such an ordinary name for the unusual things she has in stock."

"There's nothing ordinary about *her,*" said Beatrice Parker. "She gives me the willies."

Even though the shop looked dim and dingy from the street, it always drew customers. They were fascinated by the unique displays in the windows.

Agnes was polite, but she kept to herself. While people wanted to do business with her, none of them wanted her for a friend.

She never did anything to offend anyone, but there was something about her that held them at a distance. It was more than the unpleasant fragrance that sometimes filled the shop and clung to Agnes Deverell, even when she was on the street. It was the way she looked at them.

"I felt like that woman had an evil eye on me from the minute I entered the shop," Charlotte told the ladies at the church sewing guild.

"You were actually in her shop?" asked Beatrice. "I've always felt too skittish to go in."

"I was nervous," admitted Charlotte, "but I got the idea that she might buy some of the things that we sew here at church. I thought it wouldn't do any harm to ask, so I went in to see her. She wasn't interested, though."

"Did she say why?" asked Beatrice.

"Not really," said Charlotte.

"I don't see why she wouldn't like our things," said Beatrice. "Our sewing is as good as any of that handmade stuff on her shelves."

"Well, that was the odd part," said Charlotte. "I could tell that she really liked the samples I took in, but as soon as I mentioned that we made them here at church, she said she was sorry she couldn't use them. Then she hurried me right out of the shop.

"How rude!" exclaimed Beatrice.

"To tell you the truth, I was glad to go," said Charlotte. "There was an extremely unpleasant odor in there. She said she was dehydrating some fruit, but it smelled like burning sulfur to me."

"Did she have a black cat?" laughed Beatrice.

Charlotte laughed, too.

"Not that I saw," she said. "But I half expected one to pounce on me!"

The other ladies spent the next few minutes asking Charlotte details of her visit. Everyone had an odd bit to contribute about the strange old lady in the craft shop.

"If you ask me," said Charlotte, "I think Agnes Deverell dabbles in a craft more ancient than the arts and crafts displayed in her shop."

The ladies nodded their agreement.

"A woman like that doesn't belong here," said Beatrice. "That craft shop should be put out of business! That old witch could put a curse on the whole town."

After that meeting, the rumor spread quickly that the frail little proprietor practiced a sinister art in the back room behind the craft shop.

Agnes Deverell didn't need three guesses to figure out who had started the whole thing. She watched the ladies from the sewing group eye the shop with keen interest every time they walked by. They would smile smugly at each other unless Agnes appeared. Then they'd almost run to get away without so much as a nod in her direction. Agnes laughed every time she saw them.

"They've started to believe their own gossip," she said to herself.

Eventually, the gossip took its toll on Agnes Deverell's business. Many stopped to look in the windows, but fewer and fewer people came into the shop to buy.

She could see people whispering and pointing at her, and she knew they believed she really was a witch. When a stone came crashing through her window one morning, Agnes knew it was time to take action!

She had a quota to fill before closing the shop, and she thought she had a way to do it. She talked to her superior, and they agreed that a going-out-of-business sale was her best course to follow. She would take what she could get here and then move to a new location.

Agnes put her sale sign in the window, and a few customers ventured in. She appreciated the sales, but what she really wanted was a little time with the two women who had stirred up all this trouble for her. She had dealt with people like them before, and she knew exactly what to do.

Agnes stood in the doorway of her shop one morning as Beatrice and Charlotte walked by on their way to the sewing session at the church. Agnes had timed it right.

"Excuse me, ladies," said Agnes. "I wonder if you would come inside for a moment. I have some items I'd like you to have, since I'm going out of business."

Charlotte and Beatrice glanced uneasily at each other, shocked that this woman would have the gall to speak to them.

"Thank you," said Charlotte, "but we don't have any money with us today."

"I don't want any money," said Agnes. "These are just some things that you and the other ladies in your sewing circle can use."

Agnes smiled graciously at them from the doorway.

Charlotte and Beatrice held a whispered consultation. They both felt a little guilty about starting the rumor that the old woman was a witch.

"It wouldn't hurt to stop a minute," said Charlotte. "She can't hurt us if we're together!"

"And she is offering us something for nothing," added Beatrice.

They both smiled at Agnes and followed her inside the shop. The smell of something burning greeted them when they walked through the door.

"Come on back into my sitting room," said Agnes. "I was hoping to catch you, so I've got the kettle on for tea. Do have a cup with me while I gather up your things for you!"

Agnes opened the door to her living quarters behind the little shop. A fire was crackling in an old wood stove. The teakettle began to whistle as they came in. Agnes took tea bags from a hand-painted canister, placed them in dainty cups, and poured the boiling water over them. The aroma of the tea rose from the cups, and Beatrice and Charlotte couldn't resist drinking the beverage.

With every sip, Charlotte and Beatrice felt better and better about coming in. They both accepted refills when Agnes offered.

As they drank the second cup, the room began to look different. Flames from the old stove leaped around the walls. The plain black dress that Agnes wore changed to a flowing robe.

Charlotte and Beatrice thought they saw somebody else come into the room, but when they compared notes later, they felt they must have been mistaken. They had both seen a dark figure, but she was wearing a silly hat with horns!

Neither Beatrice nor Charlotte could actually remember leaving the back room. They found themselves outside again, walking down the street. Each was holding a special handmade broom and some of the delicious tea that Agnes had given them from the craft shop.

"Charlotte," complained Beatrice, "my eyes are burning!"

"Mine, too," said Charlotte. "It was really hot in there!"

"I don't feel like going to the meeting at church today," said Beatrice. "I couldn't sew a thing the way my head aches. I think I'll go on home."

"Me, too," said Charlotte. "I don't want to show them my broom just yet, either."

"Right!" said Beatrice. "All in good time!"

They both laughed as if they had done something very funny, but neither of them understood why.

Agnes watched from her shop as the two women walked down the street, and then she turned back to her business. In a big black book marked CONVERSIONS, she carefully entered the names of Charlotte Colter and Beatrice Parker. She felt good about filling her quota.

She took one last glance at the two women as they parted on the street corner, carrying their brooms. The art would come easy to both of them. They weren't as refined as she was, but it wouldn't take them long to master the craft.

Bone Diggers

Lori Simmons didn't really want to babysit for the Wilsons that Friday night. Even though they lived on a quiet street in a respectable neighborhood, Lori felt uneasy there for several reasons.

It bothered her that the Wilsons sometimes argued in front of her. Mrs. Wilson always seemed nervous and worried that her dog, Digger, would do something to set her husband off. Mr. Wilson didn't like dogs—especially if they lived in the house. Lori felt the Wilsons had little in common except their young son.

What disturbed her the most was the fact that her friend Barbara, who lived on that street, had disappeared last year and no trace of her had ever been found.

In spite of her misgivings, Lori felt she owed the Wilsons a favor. They had hired her to babysit their little boy Danny when she'd needed to earn extra money for school.

"My wife and I have to attend a very important business dinner," Mr. Wilson had said when he called. "We'll be back early, and the neighbors will be home."

Lori knew all the neighbors. Old Mrs. Watson lived on one side, ever since her daughter had died in another town. The Ballards were a middle-aged couple who lived on the other side. It was their daughter who had disappeared. She could count on them if she ever needed any help.

"I'll leave Digger inside to keep you company," offered Mr. Wilson.

Lori knew that was a big concession on his part. Digger did have a way of getting into mischief. She liked to have him around, though, because he always barked at strangers. That made her feel safe.

Considering all these positive things, Lori had agreed to take the job.

Once she'd accepted, she began to feel better. She even began to look forward to it.

"I can use the extra money," she told herself, "and the evening won't be dull with Digger around."

This might even help her deal with her loss of Barbara. She should have gone with her to sell candy for school that night last year, but she'd had to stay home and study for a test. She never saw Barbara again.

Lori arrived at the Wilsons' house on Friday a little before six. She said hello to Mrs. Watson, who was cutting a bouquet of roses.

"Babysitting tonight?" asked the old lady.

"Yes, Mrs. Watson," replied Lori.

"Call if you need anything," said Mrs. Watson, going inside with her roses.

"Thanks, I will," Lori called after her.

As she turned up the walk, Lori could see the Ballards in their living room, reading the evening paper in front of the window. They had changed so much since Barbara's disappearance! They looked so lonely now. She felt guilty that she hadn't visited them, but she didn't know how to say how very sorry she was. She knew how much they must miss Barbara. She missed her, too.

Barbara used to come over and keep her company when she babysat for Danny. She'd asked Barbara once why she didn't want the job since it was so close by, but Barbara said she didn't want to be alone there. She never did explain why.

The Wilsons were ready to go when Lori arrived. Little Danny was already asleep. Digger looked at her from his favorite place by the chair, thumped his tail, and went to sleep, too.

"Danny will probably stay asleep until we get back," said Mrs. Wilson.

The Wilsons left, and Lori sat down in the big chair to watch TV. A scary movie that she'd been wanting to see was on tonight. As she watched, she heard all the creaks and odd noises that all houses make as soon as someone is alone.

"I've got to control my imagination," Lori thought. "This scary movie will have me thinking all sorts of things."

It was too exciting to turn off, so she reached over and patted Digger's head, and he roused up and watched, too.

The longer Lori sat watching the show, the more she felt that someone was watching *her* through the drawn patio curtains. Once when the screen was silent, she heard something out there. She was sure it was footsteps.

Digger was listening, too, but he was quiet. That made her feel better. He'd be barking if somebody strange was prowling around.

"I hope the Wilsons stopped leaving a key out on the patio," thought Lori.

When a commercial came on, Lori went to the kitchen to make a sandwich. She remembered how she and Barbara used to stuff themselves while they watched scary movies. She wished she could know what happened to Barbara.

As Lori opened and closed the refrigerator, she thought the patio door opened and closed quietly, too. She felt like bolting out the back door and running for help, but she forced herself to look into the living room. She heard a soft thump that sounded familiar.

"It's Digger thumping his tail," she laughed.

She checked the patio door just to be certain, and it was securely locked.

Lori poured herself a coke, grabbed her sandwich, and rushed back to the living room just as the movie came back on. For the next few minutes, she sat completely absorbed in it. Digger went back to sleep close to the patio door.

During the commercial, Lori went back to the kitchen to clean up after her snack. She wiped off the tray she'd used and ran water to rinse her glass. As she turned the faucet off, she heard something walking in the living room.

"Digger must be awake," she said aloud.

The soft footsteps crossed to the stairs. Lori was sure of it. But why would Digger be going upstairs?

She didn't think she had the courage to look this time, but she made herself do it. There was nothing there.

"If Barbara were around, I'd swear she was playing tricks on me," thought Lori.

She wished she had someone to talk to. She was getting a bad case of the jitters.

The phone rang at that same instant and Lori nearly screamed at the sudden noise.

It was her mother calling to see if everything was all right.

"I'm fine," Lori assured her. "Just a little jumpy."

"Are the neighbors home?" inquired her mother.

"Yes," said Lori, "but I think the Ballards have gone to bed. Mrs. Watson told me to call if I need anything."

"I wouldn't count too much on that poor old thing," her mother advised. "After her daughter died, Mrs. Watson used to get confused and call Barbara by her daughter's name. Mrs. Wilson says she forgets and leaves the gate open and then complains if Digger gets into her roses."

"Don't worry about me," said Lori.

"Call if you need us," said her mother.

She hung up, feeling much better. The feeling didn't last but a few seconds. Right above her head was a terrible noise she couldn't identify:

Bump! Bump! Bump! Bump! Bump!

"It's Danny!" she thought. "He must have fallen out of bed!"

She ran from the kitchen, raced up the stairs two at a time, and jerked open the nursery door. From the sound of the bumping, she had expected to see the little boy sprawled on the floor or some mysterious intruder bent on harming him. There was neither. Danny was sleeping peacefully in his bed.

Through the open window came the strong scent of Mrs. Watson's roses. Lori ran to the window to see if someone had tried to climb inside, but there was nothing to indicate that. There was no breeze to blow anything down. Nothing in the room was out of place.

"What could have made a noise like that and disappeared? A ghost?" she asked aloud.

She regretted she'd asked the question. The window fell by itself with a bang and the room grew icy cold. Even though her eyes told her otherwise, she had the unshakable feeling that she and Danny were not the only ones in the room. She promised herself that after tonight, she'd never, ever babysit here again.

She forced herself to look in each room and closet before she left Danny in his bed and went downstairs. No wonder Barbara had never wanted to be alone here.

She was nearly to the bottom step when the noise started again right beside her.

Bump! Bump! Bump! Bump! Bump!

"Why isn't Digger barking?" she thought. "He's got to be able to hear this! Maybe he does hear it, but maybe it's familiar! Maybe it's just pipes banging somewhere in the house."

When she reached the bottom step, the scent of roses filled the house.

There was nothing out of place downstairs, so she must be right about the noise coming from the plumbing.

Digger stretched and yawned and looked up at her. Then he walked to the patio door and scratched to get out.

Lori pulled the curtain and looked out. Nothing was moving in the yard. She opened the door and let Digger out, instructing him to make his bathroom break a short one.

She waited by the door, but Digger did not return. She called to him just as she heard Mrs. Watson's voice, shrill and angry.

"Get out of my roses, you bad dog! Get!"

Before Lori could call again, Digger raced by her with something in his mouth. Lori turned to apologize to Mrs. Watson, but her door slammed shut.

Lori gave her attention to Digger to see what he'd dragged into the house. He was in front of the TV again, guarding his new possession between his paws.

"What have you got there, Digger?" Lori asked.

Digger gave an obligatory growl as she took it from him and examined it. It was a bone of some kind. She never had seen one like it, but it must have been buried in Mrs. Watson's rose garden for some time. Perhaps she should call Mrs. Watson and apologize for letting Digger out. As she reached for the phone, it rang. This time it was Mr. Wilson calling.

"Is everything all right, Lori? My wife wanted me to check on Danny," he said.

"Danny's fine," said Lori. "Digger is in a bit of trouble with Mrs. Watson, though. When I let him out for the bathroom, he dug up one of his bones from her flower bed. I don't think she was happy that he was in her roses. I was just going to call and apologize."

"Don't bother. I'll take care of it," he said. "We'll be home soon."

Lori thought his voice sounded funny. She hoped he wouldn't be angry. It probably would be better to let him handle it. It really wasn't any of her business anyway.

She sat on the floor by Digger and looked at the bone again. It looked like one from her biology book. She and Barbara had studied biology together just last year.

Bump!Bump!Bump!Bump!Bump!

The sounds came rapidly together. The air was filled with the smell of roses again.

All she could think of was Barbara!

"I must be going crazy," she thought. "Here I am sitting on the floor looking at a ... a human bone that a dog dug up from a rose garden, and I'm thinking of Barbara."

What she was thinking just couldn't be true! She didn't believe in ghosts, but maybe Barbara was trying to tell her something. The bumping must be a warning. If it was, then this bone must be from Barbara's arm! She nearly fainted from the thought. The bone had come from Mrs. Watson's rose garden. That meant that Mrs. Watson had killed Barbara and buried her under the roses! No wonder she didn't want Digger digging there!

A light flashed under the patio curtains. Lori crawled over and peeked out. Mrs. Watson's porch light was on and Lori could see the old woman bent over her roses with a flashlight in one hand and a small garden spade in the other.

Then she turned and ran toward the Wilsons' front door. Mrs. Watson rang the bell, but Lori sat very still and didn't answer. It rang again and again, but Lori continued to sit perfectly still.

"Maybe she'll think we're asleep and go away," hoped Lori.

At last Mrs. Watson gave up and hurried back to her house. Lori was weak with relief. She started to phone the Ballards, when she heard a key in the door. She hoped Mrs. Watson had not found a key outside. She choked back a scream as the door opened and Mr. Wilson came inside.

"I am so glad to see you!" sobbed Lori.

He listened as she told him what had happened.

"You did the right thing, Lori," he said. "Have you called anyone to come get you?"

"No," said Lori. "Is Mrs. Wilson waiting to drive me home?"

"She's in the car," said Mr. Wilson.

Lori opened the door and started out, when she heard him laugh—a low, cold laugh that she had never heard from him before. The smell of roses filled the air.

"Mrs. Wilson won't be driving you home, though," he continued.

"What are you talking about?" asked Lori. "What do you mean?"

"My wife figured everything out tonight, Lori, just like you did. Now she's dead. Just like you're going to be."

Lori didn't know she could feel such fear and still function. She started to run, but he grabbed her arm and jerked her around.

"Why did you do it?" she asked. "Why would you kill someone as sweet as Barbara?"

"I didn't mean to kill Barbara. My wife and Danny were away visiting. I was lonely. Barbara came to the door selling candy. I asked her in while I got some money. I just wanted her to be nice to me. I just wanted to touch her. She tried to scream when I put my hands on her neck. I had to make her be quiet! I took her head and I beat it against the door casing. I kept it up until she died: *Bump! Bump! Bump! Bump! Bump!* Mrs. Watson was away, too, and I was watching her house for her. I buried Barbara under the rosebushes. I didn't think anybody would ever look there."

He stopped for a minute, a faraway look in his eyes. Lori tried to pull away, but he held tighter.

"Nobody would have known if it hadn't been for you and that nosy dog!" he said. "He took the first bone to my wife, but she didn't know what it was. When she heard us on the phone tonight, she made the connection. She was going to turn me in. I had to kill her, and now I have to kill you!"

He brought his hands up toward her throat, and the door opened quietly behind him.

"Let her go!" a voice said.

He released Lori and whirled around. Mrs. Watson stood in the doorway, holding the knife she had used to cut the roses.

Mr. Wilson lunged at the old woman and grabbed her arm. She held tightly to the knife as they struggled. Lori tried to move, but a flash of fur flew by her and sprang into the air. Mr. Wilson yanked the knife from Mrs. Watson's hand as Digger sank his teeth into his master's arm. Mr. Wilson yelled with pain, staggered backwards, lost his balance, and fell on the knife. He lay silent, his eyes wide open with surprise.

Mrs. Watson came to Lori and put her arms around her.

"It's all right now, child," she said. "I called the police before I came over."

Mrs. Watson helped her to the couch, and she sat there stunned, listening to the sirens getting louder. Digger licked her face and then ran out to the officers when they arrived.

Mrs. Watson explained to a man in uniform that she had discovered more bones when she went to repair the damage Digger had done to her roses. She went to warn Lori, but Lori didn't answer the door. She called, but the line was busy. She rushed home to call the police, but she saw Mr. Wilson come back and go into the house alone. She had known then that Lori was in terrible danger, and that the police might not get there in time to save her. She grabbed her knife and ran to help. They knew the rest.

Lori's parents came to take her home. She saw a policeman putting Danny in a police car. She saw men shoveling dirt from under the rosebushes, while the Ballards stood watching and crying.

"Thank you for trying to warn me, my friend," Lori whispered to Barbara.

A gentle breeze touched Lori's face. Once more, she smelled the roses.

Feed My Cats

Big One's claws raked across the basement door that led up into Anna Eaton's kitchen.

"MEOW!" he roared.

Anna stroked her other cats as she tore open the packaged cat food and filled the bowls that lined the kitchen wall. Then she hurriedly opened small cans of turkey, salmon, and chicken, and topped the bowls with the cats' special treats. They began to gobble the food at once.

"MEOW!" Big One repeated, still scratching the door.

The meowing and the scratching on the basement door reminded Anna that her favorite cat hadn't been fed yet.

Big One didn't eat as often as the others, but his appetite was ferocious once he began to get hungry.

"Be patient, Big One!" she called. "I'll see that you get your favorite treat soon!"

Big One began to purr. Anna was glad he was happy. It wouldn't be wise to keep him waiting too long.

Anna took especially good care of her cats. She lived alone, so she had plenty of time to spoil them.

Anna knew that people talked about her, but she didn't care. She knew they said she cared more about cats than she did people, and that she spent more money on cat food than she spent on herself. She saw nothing wrong with that. Her greatest pleasure was to watch her cats eat—especially Big One.

Anna didn't know where Big One had come from. He had appeared at her door one stormy night when she was very lonely, so she'd brought him in and fed him. Since that night, he had been her closest companion, and she had taken great satisfaction in providing him with a proper diet.

She'd found out quite by accident what he preferred. It wasn't always easy to obtain the kind of food he wanted. Sometimes it required a great deal of planning and effort.

She couldn't let him out to hunt his own food. He was much too rare. Somebody might take him away from her. She kept him locked in the basement, so nobody would know he was there.

"Meow!" screeched Big One impatiently, scratching the door again.

"All right!" called Anna. "I'll arrange for your treat right now."

She hated to call on her neighbors and co-workers down at the office, especially since they had made unkind remarks to her in the past. She needed help with her cats in order to make arrangements for Big One, though, and she had no other choice.

She phoned her neighbor, Madaline Miller, first.

Madaline Miller was the only one who had ever complained about her cats getting out. That had only happened once, when Anna had left the door ajar while she carried in groceries. Two of the cats had slipped out and caught a bird. Madaline had made an awful row about it. She'd hit one of the cats with a rock. Anna hadn't forgotten!

Madaline answered after several rings.

"Madaline," Anna said, "this is Anna Eaton. I hate to impose, but there's something I simply have to do, and I was wondering if you would be kind enough to feed my cats late this afternoon."

Madaline hesitated. She didn't like cats, but she knew she hadn't been very nice to Anna that time her pets got loose. This would be a neighborly thing to do, and maybe it would make up for their differences in the past.

"Yes," said Madaline. "I can do that for you."

"You're a dear to do it," said Anna. "I'll have everything ready. The cats will be in the kitchen. Don't open the basement door. My steps are steep and dangerous. I'll leave the key under the mat on the porch. 'Bye!"

Anna rushed about preparing for what she had to do.

As soon as she hung up, Madaline was filled with misgivings. She didn't like going into the empty house alone, but she had no choice now. Anna was counting on her to feed the cats.

Late that afternoon, Madaline went to Anna's house just as she promised. She was hoping the key wouldn't be there so she would have an excuse not to go in, but it was under the mat.

As Madaline stepped inside, the cats immediately emerged from dark corners to greet her. They rubbed against her legs, eager for their dinner.

Anna had set the food out and had left written instructions. Madaline followed the instructions and opened the packages and cans and filled the bowls. The cats rushed over and began gulping down the food.

Madaline felt good about doing Anna a favor. She started to leave, but a sound from behind the basement door stopped her in her tracks.

"Meow!" Big One's voice boomed.

"I thought she left all her cats in the kitchen," Madaline said aloud.

"Meow!" she heard again, and this time, the meow was followed by frantic scratching on the door.

"Poor thing!" thought Madaline. "It smells the food and can't get to it. I'll bet Anna didn't know it was down there when she closed the door."

"Meow! Meow!" said Big One louder than ever.

"Okay, okay, I'll let you out," said Madaline. "Anna told me not to open the basement door, but I know she'd want me to feed you."

The door was unlocked, so she pulled it open. She was face to face with the biggest cat she had ever seen!

Madaline had only a second to stare at Big One. His dark, shadowy form leaped at her. She saw blazing green eyes and fiery red claws as sharp teeth tore into her flesh.

"YEOW!" screeched Big One, pouncing and pulling his prey down the basement steps to where Anna was waiting.

Anna stood among the shadows in the far corner of the basement and watched with great pleasure as Big One finished his treat. She had done what she had to do. She had bags, a mop, and a bucket of water in case she needed to clean up after Big One was through.

"They always do what they're told not to do," chuckled Anna. "I warned her not to open the basement door!"

Big One swallowed his last bite, licked his paws, and meowed at Anna for more.

"You can't still be hungry!" she said.

He licked his paws again and stared at her.

"Well, okay," said Anna, "but just one more this week. You mustn't be greedy. Let's see now. Whom shall I call?"

She ran through a mental list of names, and then remembered Edith Gorman down at the office. Edith would be perfect. Anna hadn't forgotten how she embarrassed her yesterday.

When Edith answered the phone, Anna spoke in her friendliest voice.

"Edith," she said, "this is Anna Eaton. I hate to bother you at home, but there's something I simply have to do, and I was wondering if you could stop by on your way to work in the morning and feed my cats?"

Edith was a little surprised that Anna was asking her for a favor. Just yesterday, they'd had words over an office report that Anna failed to complete properly, and she had said some unkind things to her. She'd even called her stupid. She was sorry now that she'd been so hard on her. This would be a good way to make it up to her.

"Yes," said Edith. "I can feed the cats."

"You're a dear to do it," said Anna. "I'll have everything ready. The cats will be in the kitchen. Don't open the basement door. My steps are steep and dangerous. I'll leave the key under the mat on the porch. 'Bye!"

Anna hung up the phone and hummed as she cleaned the kitchen. She gathered her bags, her mop, and her bucket and took them to the corner of the basement.

As evening shadows gathered, she turned out the upstairs lights, closed the basement door, and took her place beside Big One in the darkness. She smiled, and Big One purred softly as she stroked him.

Morning would come very soon.

Other books and tapes from
August House Publishers

Favorite Scary Stories of American Children
Twenty-three tales collected from children aged five to ten.
ISBN 0-87483-120-2, HB
ISBN 0-87483-119-9, TPB

Ghost Stories from the American Southwest
142 shivery tales gathered from the oral tradition.
ISBN 0-87483-125-3, HB
ISBN 0-87483-174-1, TPB
ISBN 0-87483-149-0, Audiocassette, 45 mins.

The Walking Trees and Other Scary Stories
Twenty-five chillers for ages 12 and up.
ISBN 0-87483-143-1, TPB

Civil War Ghosts
John Jakes, Ambrose Bierce, Vance Randolph,
Manly Wade Wellman, and other great American writers
remember the war in which everyone took sides—even the dead.
ISBN 0-87483-173-3, TPB

Cajun Ghost Stories
Five blood-chilling stories from the land of moss, magnolias, and bayous.
Winner of the 1992 Parents' Choice Award.
ISBN 0-87483-210-1, audiocassette, 68 mins.

Tales of an October Moon
Haunting stories from New England.
Winner of Audioworld's Golden Headset Award for
Best Children's Audio.
ISBN 0-87483-209-8, audiocassette, 60 mins.

The Scariest Stories Ever
For ages 12 and up.
ISBN 0-87483-253-5, audiocassette, 50 mins.

Ozark Ghost Stories
Includes traditional music and sound effects.
ISBN 0-87483-211-X, audiocassette, 45 mins.

August House Publishers
P.O. Box 3223, Little Rock, Arkansas 72203
1-800-284-8784